Contents

Peas and Princesses

Book One of *The Tales and Princesses Series*

Aleese Hughes

ISBN: 9781088534274

Dedication

To my incredible husband, who supports me 24/7, 365 days a year. Thank you for your love and for being my best friend.

Chapter 1

King Leopold held the ledgers under the candle-light. The papers scratched against his callused hands, callused from years as an experienced swordsman. His frustration built more by each second. The kingdom's financial setbacks scared him more than anything else. The always impending threats from the neighboring kingdom of Polart were draining his funds— he was constantly sending out troops to secure the borders and throwing frivolous parties to ease the minds of his subjects. He couldn't let anyone think he was weak. There was only one thing left to try in order to bring peace for Mardasia, and his daughter was a key part of that plan.

Leopold reclined back in his chair and moved his gaze to the crown that rested atop his desk. He stared at his reflection in the gold, admiring the strength and power evident in his eyes, regardless of the problems he faced. If anyone could succeed, it was him.

A light knock sounded on his study door, and he hurriedly tucked the ledgers away.

"Enter," he bellowed.

A wide-eyed, frail woman stepped in, staring at the mess of maps and books strewn across the room.

"Speak!" Leopold snapped.

She paled. "Sire…"

"Good gracious, woman! Tell me!"

She cowered a little smaller. "The princess is— is gone."

King Leopold groaned and covered his face in his hands. He heard the rustling of papers as she kicked them away, slowly trying to approach him among the mess.

"Sire?"

Leopold grabbed the closest, hardest book he could find and threw it at the woman, who fortunately dodged it just in time.

"She has ruined everything!" The king paused, accentuating the dangerous atmosphere. The nervous woman shifted from foot to foot. The king then shifted his gaze to his visitor. "You are her maid, are you not?"

Trembling, she nodded.

He let out a short chuckle. "Are you not supposed to know of her whereabouts every moment of every day?"

The short woman whimpered, inching closer to the door. "S—s—sire! I—I…"

Leopold rose from his large, pillowed chair and stepped towards her, red robes flowing behind him like a raging fire. Their faces were close, the king's brown eyes piercing into her gray. The sound of his strike across her cheek echoed loudly in the room. She fell to the floor, tears falling down her face.

"You will be the cause of this kingdom's downfall," Leopold spat.

King Leopold slid a long sword from the sheath at his waist, grinning as it glinted from the glowing candlesticks scattered across the study. The weapon felt familiar in his grip, giving him the delightful eagerness he always felt when wielding it. The woman wrapped her arms around herself and wailed hysterically, unable to control herself, rocking back and forth on her knees.

"No!" she cried between sobs. "I have a family! Please, Sire! I'll do *anything*."

Leopold shrugged as he stroked his blade. Then, without batting an eye, he ran the sword through the woman's chest. She slumped to the floor, the look of terror frozen on her white face. He smiled as he slid the weapon out from the corpse.

"Guard!" King Leopold said as he held the blood-stained sword away from his clothes.

A large man with a crooked nose quickly opened the study door and bowed to the King. The body at his feet didn't even phase him.

"Your Majesty?"

Leopold handed the sword to the man. "Clean my sword and dispose of that." He gestured to the lifeless woman dirtying his carpets with her blood.

Chapter 2

A sharp rapping on the door woke me in the dead of night.

What now, I thought.

Groaning, I pulled my warm blankets off and shivered in the cold, night air. I blindly stumbled around the cabin to look for our last candlestick. We were always running dangerously low on everything, including candles.

The knocking sounded again.

"I'm coming!"

I hissed as I lit the wick on the pathetic stub of wax, nearly burning myself. Light in hand, I tiptoed across the wooden floor, careful not to wake my older sister Janice resting on the other side of the room.

"Who would come knocking at this hour?" I muttered under my breath.

Not knowing what to expect, I pulled the door open, ready to reprimand our untimely visitor. A hooded figure stood before me, face hidden from the shadows. Before I could say anything, the visitor pushed past me and into the room.

"Hey!" I shouted, slamming the door. "What do

you think you're doing, barging into someone's home like that?"

Janice shot up from her mattress, eyes wide in fear, and her mousy-brown hair sticking up in messy tangles. "Milly, what's wrong?" Her eyes shifted to the mysterious person standing right in front of her. "Who are *you*?"

I folded my arms, trying to make my tiny, feminine body look intimidating. "That's what I'd like to know!"

The figure pulled away the hood in one quick motion. I gasped as the long, blonde curls fell around her shoulders and recognized the face immediately. I had only seen her once before, while in the capital Capthar, and it was at a significant distance, but it was definitely her.

"Your Highness!" I shouted as I fell to my knees.

"Hush!" Princess Amelia hissed at me. "I can't be found!" She pulled me to my feet. "And there's no need for kneeling—not anymore, anyway." She ran to the windows, hurriedly shutting the drapes, then followed with locking the front and back doors.

"Princess?" Janice said. My sister was a very reserved person and had never actually left our little town of Marviton before, so she wouldn't know what the Princess looked like. And beyond that, the royal family didn't make many appearances, especially not in peasant towns like ours.

I nodded to my sister and watched curiously as the Princess paced our cabin. Why was she here?

"Um, Princess?" I said.

"Please don't call me that!" she snapped.

Janice and I exchanged glances. "Um… Amelia… why are you here?"

Amelia rubbed her porcelain face with her hands. She seemed exhausted. "I need your help," she choked. She caught herself before her watered eyes spilled over and straightened her back. Clearing her throat, she continued, "There are search parties after me, and your…" She paused, looking around our cabin with a hint of disgust, "…home, as you called it, is the furthest from the castle. I've been running all night— I need provisions and a horse, if you have one. I can pay you right now for it." She walked over to our small table, pulled out a purse hidden under her dark cloak and poured out a few handfuls of gold pieces.

I couldn't help but laugh. "What?"

"I need to sit down," my sister said as she moved to the fireplace.

"Please," the Princess pleaded. "They'll catch up to me any minute."

I shook my head. "Your Highness, I—"

"Amelia."

I sighed. "Amelia, what is going on?"

She stared at me with her pretty brown eyes, tears starting to appear again. I recognized the desperation in her gaze and all of a sudden, she seemed helpless. I found myself wanting to help her.

I nodded. "I'll start putting together some food

for you. Hey, Jan? Will you saddle up Tuff?"

Janice nodded and ran to unlock the back door.

"Tuff is our only horse," I said, hurriedly throwing some apples and dried meat into a sack.

Amelia nodded. "The money should cover it."

I handed her the food and led her out back. The Princess's eyes darted back and forth, searching our small garden and squinting past the little wagon we had. She shifted her gaze to Janice as she untied our horse from the splintered post.

"This is Tuff," I said as Janice handed the reins to the Princess.

Amelia stroked his brown coat, whispering things to him I could not hear. The Princess swung her leg over him with ease. A sudden sadness rushed over me as I watched Tuff whinny happily for the chance of a ride— we'd been through a lot with that horse. Amelia pulled the reins in her hand and turned her head to us. "Thank you. I will never forget this."

She dug her heels into the sides of the horse, and he bolted away. We watched as her cloak billowed behind her, and the dust Tuff kicked up from the dirt road began to obscure our view as the Princess rode further away.

"Wow," Janice whispered under her breath. "That was... interesting."

Shivering, I nodded.

Chapter 3

It had been two days since my encounter with the Princess Amelia, and it was very hard to forget it. Thoughts kept spinning in my head about *why* she had run away, *why* we hadn't seen anyone looking for her. It was actually rather mysterious.

I turned my attention to my surroundings, breathing in deeply through my nose. Marviton was beautiful in the fall, with the deep red and orange leaves decorating the trees along my path. The scenery on the way to Bart's store was breathtaking. I smiled as the sun's warmth spread across my tan face.

Looking ahead, I saw the old man sweeping the porch front of his store. Bart's was Marviton's one place to buy all types of odds and ends things. Like food, furniture, and the thing I needed: a new horse.

"Hey, Bart!"

Bart halted mid-sweep. "Milly, what a pleasant surprise!" he shouted back at me as I ran up to him.

I smiled at the round man. He had always been like an uncle to Janice and me, having been a good friend of our mother's, and watching over us since her death.

"How's business, Barty?"

He put his broom down. "It's been slow today. I've actually had time to sweep my porch, as you can see." He gestured to the broom against the wall. "Hey, you should see something I found during my most recent travels!"

When Bart wasn't tending to his store, he was always exploring other kingdoms and picking up new souvenirs to show off and sell to his customers. I always enjoyed hearing his stories.

"I'd love to." I smiled, excited to see what he had.

Bart gestured for me to follow him inside, bouncing up and down eagerly. I did, and breathed in the sweet aroma of things like wood and chocolate. The walls were aligned with intriguing carvings, sacks of food, and exotic spices. It was chaotic and unorganized, but it was always such a thrilling atmosphere. I grinned at the jade figurine of a mermaid resting on a counter next to me. He got it from a distant kingdom named Wilaldan maybe three or four years ago. He had stopped all passersby that year to animatedly tell them of Wilaldan's sparkling blue oceans and *swore* he had seen the tail of a mermaid before the creature was startled and swam away from him. No one ever believed his tales, but they were always fun to hear.

"Milly, come here," he whispered.

I walked away from the beautiful figurine and found Bart in the corner edge of the room staring at a small, tattered book. The leather cover was falling off of its binding, and the golden lettering on the front had all but faded away.

"The Book of Mag?" I questioned, trying to read the cover.

"Magic," Bart said.

I cocked my head, trying not to laugh. "What? Magic's not real, Barty."

His brown eyes sparkled with a determined intensity. He grinned, licking his lips.

"I saw it, Milly." He tenderly opened the book and ran his finger down the inside. Foreign symbols and drawings covered the pages.

I raised an eyebrow at a particular image of an old man with a long beard holding a bird over a deep cauldron. Magic was the sort of thing that only existed in children's stories.

"I saw this warlock in the Edristan Kingdom not far north of the Polart Kingdom. He healed a little boy's broken leg right before my eyes! And then he told my future." Bart stood up straighter, seemingly proud of himself. "He told me that within the next two years, I would meet and marry the most beautiful woman I would ever set eyes on."

I snorted, trying to hold in another laugh. He eyed me, annoyed. Bart was a great, wonderful man, but everybody in Marviton knew he wasn't the marrying type. It might have had a little to do with the odor...

"It could happen!" he snapped.

I nodded, the corners of my lips twitching. "Of

course."

Bart huffed for a few seconds, then shrugged it off. "Hey, did you hear the rumor?"

Leave it to old Barty to have all the gossip. "What rumor?"

"The one that says the Princess went missing a couple days ago!"

Trying to seem surprised, I replied, "Where'd you hear that?"

"It's all over town! I'm surprised you haven't heard it yourself!"

"I've been at home the past few days harvesting the crop I need to sell in Capthar," I said nonchalantly.

Bart shrugged. "Well, I thought you'd like to hear what's been happenin'. Some versions of the story say she ran away with a servant boy."

That one surprised me. "Really?"

He chuckled. "Pretty scandalous stuff, eh?"

Servant boy, I thought. *I didn't see anyone with her... Was she trying to meet him somewhere?*

"The royals are pretty strange, though... No one ever really sees King Leopold and the Princess, unless you're a noble at one of their ridiculous parties." Bart clenched his fists in a sudden anger. "That's a waste of money, in my opinion."

The royals *did* seem more frivolous than they should be. I was under the impression that they were just throwing all their money away on unimportant things like parties and their own comfort — never concerning themselves with the lives of the commoners.

"So, what brings you to my place today?" Bart said, pulling me out of my reverie.

"Well, like I said, I need to go into Capthar, but I am lacking a horse."

Bart raised an eyebrow. "What happened to Tuff? I sold him to you not even three months ago!"

I brushed his accusations away. "He must've run away. He wasn't tied securely enough to our post, I guess."

Bart put his chubby fists on his hips sternly, cheeks turning red. "Mildred Wallander! You know better than to be losin' your horse like that! I hope you have the money to pay for a new one!"

"Of course I do," I shot back at him. "Jan and I have been saving." My cheeks turned red from the lie. It was more like we'd been *given* money by a runaway princess.

He let out a big puff of air. "Fine. Let's go to the back."

Bart led me to the stables, muttering profanities under his breath. "Losing a horse," he huffed. "Your father would've never done such a thing."

I stopped in my tracks and thought of my wretched father. Bart noticed I had stopped and turned to me, face softening.

"I'm sorry, Milly. I wasn't thinking."

I un-clenched my fists. Father... I actually hadn't thought of him in days. All this princess business had taken my mind off of a lot of things.

Bart gestured towards all the horses standing behind their gates, neighing and clopping their hooves with excitement. "Any specific horse you're looking for?"

"Which is your best?"

He raised an eyebrow. "Think you can afford something so expensive?"

"Like I said, we've been saving."

Bart looked at me suspiciously, then led me to the last gate in the small stable. "This is Borden," he said. "Young and firey, but loyal, strong, and fast."

Borden was a beautiful horse— dark as night, and his strong muscles pulsed under his shiny coat.

I nodded. "How much?"

He hesitated. "Ten gold pieces and three silver."

"Hmm…" I said. "I think you can do better than that."

Barty raised an eyebrow. "You were always quite the negotiator." He stroked the scruff on his chin, feigning an inner turmoil. "I'll do ten gold even, but that's as low as I'll go."

I smirked. "Nine."

Bart chuckled. "Deal."

I rummaged through my ragged side purse, careful not to let Barty see all the money that *was* in there. I counted out nine gold coins and held them out to the man.

"Wow, you weren't kidding about your savings," he said as he snatched the money from my hand. "He's all yours."

Janice walked up to me and watched as I tied the new horse to our post. She stroked his nose gently. "Hey there, buddy," she whispered, brown hair falling in front of her face.

My sister was older than I by two years and definitely the pretty one with her glowing skin and shining, green eyes. But I was the strong one. When our mother died three years before— Jan was 18, and I 16– our drunken father disappeared soon after. I *had* to be the strong one. My poor sister was stricken with grief that took more than a year to even *begin* to subside, and someone still had to earn the money. My anger towards our father overcame any sadness I ever felt, so I took over tending Father's small garden and orchard in our land and proceeded to sell the fruits and vegetables in our Kingdom's capital, Capthar, periodically.

"What's his name?" Jan asked.

"Borden," I said, picking up a brush to groom him. "He's the best Barty had."

Jan nodded. "How much?"

"Nine pieces."

She looked shocked. "That's not even half of what…" she paused, looking around, even though our little farm was rather far from any sort of neighbor. She then continued in a whisper, "*she* gave us."

"I negotiated him down. He actually said ten and three silver, but I wasn't having it."

Janice smiled. "It's nice having some money to spend…"

"It really is. Is there anything I can get you while I'm up there for business?"

Her smile grew bigger. "Do you think I can get a new book, with the extra money and all?"

I laughed. Janice *loved* reading. "Of course. How much do you think we've got to sell this time?"

"I picked a few dozen pumpkins, a bushel of cucumbers, *lots* of carrots and cabbage heads, and a barrel of apples," she said, gesturing towards the produce she had stacked by the back door.

"Great!" I said. "Wanna help me load up the wagon?"

Within the next half hour, we had the wagon loaded and Borden hitched. Janice wrapped me up in a hug.

"I'll be back by the end of this week," I said. Capthar was about two days north of us, Marviton being the furthest town away from the capital within our small kingdom of Mardasia.

Jan released me from her embrace and watched as I jumped into the driver's seat of the wagon. "Be safe," she whispered.

I winked. "Always am."

Chapter 4

"Miss! Miss!"

I pulled on Borden's reins and squinted past the sunlight to look to my left. Not far from me was a crippled, old woman with little gray hair left on her scalp. The skin on her face sagged past her chin, and I tried not to gag as she flashed her rotted teeth at me in a smile. She lounged on a large pile of red and orange leaves as she waved to me.

"Do you think you can help me, miss?" Her voice croaked with age, but the smile never left her face.

I hesitated. "What do you need help with?"

"I was wondering if you had any food to spare for a poor, old lady."

I glanced over my shoulder at the produce in my wagon, then back to her. I felt a pang of sympathy as I watched the woman pull her ratted shawl back over her shoulders and shiver against the cold, fall air. It wouldn't hurt to give her an apple or two.

I smiled at the woman. "Give me one second."

I led Borden and the wagon next to the tree the woman sat beside. She watched eagerly as I hopped from my seat and tied his reins around the small trunk.

"No one ever stops for me!" The woman leapt from her place and rushed towards the food. I held my hands out to stop her.

"Please," I said. "I still have to sell most of it. Let me get it for you."

She covered her mouth with her knobby, dry fingers and giggled.

"Of course." She danced back to her spot and plopped down with a thud. Leaves sprung up all around her.

I pulled two shiny, red apples from their basket and walked over to the woman. Her smell became more and more pungent the nearer I came. With a closer look, I could tell she hadn't bathed in a long time. She bounced up and down and clapped her hands together in excitement, much like an eager child.

I held out the fruit to her. "I hope this helps."

She snatched the apples from my hand and dove into them like an animal. Pieces of it flew around, and some of the juice hit me in the eye. I chuckled, uncomfortable.

"Well, I'd better get going," I said, rubbing at my eye.

The woman gasped, chucking the two cores behind her back. She had eaten those *really* fast.

"Oh, no. Please, child." She patted the spot next to her. "Will you keep me company just for a minute or two?"

I gulped. "I really do have a lot of travel today."

The woman stuck her chapped, bottom lip out in a pout. "I just wanted to talk for a second or two. Like I said, no one ever stops for me." She flashed another gruesome smile at me. "I'd like to get to know someone as special as you."

I glanced at Borden. He munched peacefully at the grass. I then looked up at the sky. There were still a few hours of sunlight left. Besides, what harm could come from talking to a frail, old woman for just a moment?

I moved to sit by her, trying not to crinkle my nose from the odor. I hugged my knees and stared out at the dirt road. There were not many travellers today, and I enjoyed the quiet. The sound of the wind rustling through the trees and the crisp air were relaxing.

"What's your name, child?" The woman sat back on her hands and closed her eyes to the warm rays of the sun.

"Milly," I replied.

She nodded. "That's what I thought."

I found myself laughing. "Lucky guess? What's your name?"

She paused for a moment and furrowed her brow. "I'm not sure which name I'm using as of this moment."

I waited a few seconds as the woman searched her mind in turmoil for what seemed, at least to me, to be an easy answer to an easy question. She was crazy.

She snapped her fingers suddenly. "Bavmorda!

That's what I've been going by lately." Bavmorda closed her eyes again, pleased with herself.

"Oh." I inched myself a little further away from her.

"You know," Bavmorda said, twirling a piece of her tattered hair around her finger, "I was almost expecting you today."

I raised an eyebrow and looked at the woman. "What do you mean by that?"

She ignored my question. "Were you able to help the Princess get away?"

I shot up from my seat and stared at her. "How did you—"

Bavmorda laid all the way back and chuckled up at me. "I pose no threat to you, child. And I will repay you for your kindness, Mildred Wallander. I promise."

I gasped as she said my full name and turned to run from the woman. Her high-pitched cackles pierced my ears as I shakily untied Borden and leapt back into the wagon. I turned my head for one last look as I quickly moved back on the road, but she was gone. It was like she had completely vanished, leaving nothing behind but the two apple cores.

Chapter 5

I stood behind my makeshift booth piled up with the produce Janice had picked for me. It didn't happen often, but this time I got a spot to set up shop in the middle of Capthar's town square. But my thoughts kept revolving around my encounter with Bavmorda two days ago, and the things she knew. She had said that she was not a threat to me, but I couldn't help but feel paranoid about being turned in for helping the Princess escape. But what had the woman meant about repaying me for my kindness?

I shook my head, determined not to think of the strange woman anymore, and turned my attention to my surroundings. Loads of people from snooty nobles to dirty street urchins bustled about, mostly ignoring me and the other merchants shouting out our various advertisements. The sounds were loud, but I found them welcoming. The smells were a mixture of things, some pleasant, some not so much: the bakery next to me provided the sweet smells of dough rising and, contrastingly, the pungent smell of body odor was strong in a big place like this.

I propped my elbows on the wood of my booth and found myself staring at the looming towers of the castle just two or three miles away, thinking about the Princess. What was she doing? Was she okay? Something about helping her that night made me see her in a different light than my past perceptions of a snobbish royal. I hoped that she was okay.

"Did you hear the news?"

I turned my head to listen to some young girls talking near me.

"They still haven't found the Princess! They say she ran off with a handsome servant. Isn't that romantic?!" The girls started giggling and skipped away.

That's the second time I heard that she ran off with a boy, I thought, definitely curious.

A little old man stepped up to my booth, interrupting my thoughts. "Hello, young lady," he croaked.

"Patrick," I said with a kind smile. "It's good to see you again! How's the wife?"

The sweet man smiled back at me, eyes crinkling with a thousand wrinkles. "Gladys is feeling a lot better. Her broken wrist is healing up very quickly."

"That is so good to hear!"

"How much for two carrots and—" he stopped to count on his fingers: "five apples?"

"Two copper," I said, putting the produce in his outstretched basket. He handed me the money, winking as he put an extra copper in my hand, and hobbled away.

It was starting to get dark, so I began counting the money I had earned in the day. There was more than enough for a night's stay in an inn and the trip home, plus a good amount of profit. It was definitely better than normal. I decided to call it a day and packed up all the leftover produce into the wagon, excited about the few pumpkins left and looking forward to making a couple pies with Janice once I got home.

"Alright, Borden," I whispered to my horse. "Let's head home."

I hopped into the driver's seat of my wagon and began to navigate through the busy traffic in the square. Navigating past the tall, stone buildings and many people was a challenge. After making it out into the town's cobblestone road, a young woman with ratted, red hair ran right in front of me.

"Hey!" I shouted, pulling the reins on Borden. "Watch where you're going!"

She stumbled over, shouting out in pain. She looked up at me, terrified, but something told me it wasn't because I had almost hit her. She hobbled off the road and made her way into a dark alleyway. Looking to my right, I saw an inn and pulled over. I tied Borden and my wagon to a post and called over the nearby stable boy.

"Will you please watch over my wagon?" I asked, pressing a copper piece into his palm.

"Sure, ma'am," the grungy boy said.

I then ran after the girl, hoping to catch up with her and help. I didn't have to go far. I found her huddled in the alleyway, clutching her ankle.

"Are—"

She lifted her finger to her mouth, shushing me, then gestured for me to come closer. Tears were welling up in her eyes as she nervously looked around. I shuffled closer to her. She was very dirty, obviously poor, but also very pretty. She must've been about the same age as me.

"Can you please help me?" she said, grabbing my shoulder. "They're after me."

"Who's after you?" I asked.

"Two men from the royal guard," she hissed through the pain in her ankle.

"What did you do?"

She shook her head vigorously. "I don't know! They found me this morning sleeping in the street. I somehow was able to get away, but they've been looking for me ever since."

I searched her eyes and found no lies there. Similarly to the Princess a few nights ago, this poor girl just look scared and helpless.

"Did you hurt your ankle?" I asked.

"Yeah. I don't know if I can walk."

"You'll have to try," I said. "Put your arm around me."

She did, and I helped her up.

"Do you think you can make it back to my wagon?"

"No!" she said. "They're coming that way! They aren't far behind me!"

"Okay," I said. "Let's find you someplace to hide."

I helped her through the alleyway as quickly as I could, all the while looking for somewhere or something to hide her in.

"You there!" a gruff voice shouted.

I whirled my head around and saw two soldiers dressed in the royal red and blue heading towards us.

"Oh no!" the young woman whimpered.

We both tried to run, but we made it maybe five feet before I felt a tug on my long hair.

One of the guards grabbed me around the waist and the other pulled the young woman off of me. I struggled against the big man as much as my tiny body could as my hands were tied. I shouted, hoping anyone could hear. The guards roughly placed a gag over my mouth to stifle my cries.

"Borge, are you sure no one's going to notice these two gone?" the guard holding my companion asked the other.

"No one's going to miss two cretins from the street, Jared," my guard spat back. "We're just doing what they ordered us to!"

"What?" I tried to shout through my gag. My stomach churned violently as I tried to process what was happening.

"I know we've been following the red-head, but how do we know this other one isn't going to be missed?" the one named Jared asked, gesturing to me.

"People go missing all the time. Besides, she's seen too much. We have to take her, too. Now grab yours and let's get out of here without drawing too much attention to ourselves. We'll take the back roads to the castle."

The castle? I thought, still struggling.

Borge threw me over his shoulder, which caused the coin purse in my pocket to fall to the ground. I watched as all my hard-earned money spilled along the cobblestones.

"Ooh," Borge said, leaning down to gather my money. I groaned as the blood started rushing to my head.

Jared moaned. "What if someone asks what we're doing?"

"We're royal guards, Jared! We can just tell them that we're arresting criminals."

Jared shrugged and leaned down to gather some of the money, as well. I watched sadly as they stole my money, all the while dangling the other girl and me over their shoulders like sacks of potatoes.

After finding every last coin, the men started running, one behind the other, the alleyway being too narrow to run side by side. They took some interesting twists and turns in the alleyways, our heads banging against the men's backs uncomfortably as they ran. I was too much in shock to feel the pain. The girl I had been trying to help gave me a petrified look. I'm sure the look I gave back was the same. Soon we made it to what must have been the "back roads" Borge was talking about. Borge thrust me onto a horse, and Jared did the same with his captive. Both men leapt behind us onto their respective horses. Tears spilled from my eyes as Borge kicked his horse, the situation finally hitting me. What had I gotten myself into?

Chapter 6

I found myself locked in a large room of the castle with three other girls. It seemed as if we were in a library— I had never seen so many books in my life, and the furniture was magnificent with gold inlays on the armrests and plush pillows scattered all over. All of the girls were whispering nervously. Soldiers surrounded us on every side, each with longswords and daggers resting in their belts.

"Why are we here?" a young woman whispered close to me. I turned to look at her and noticed she was the red-headed girl I had tried to help. I shrugged, which was surprisingly hard, considering how much my body shook from fear.

"By the way, my name's Laura." She forced a smile as she extended her hand out to me.

I hesitated. Was it really the time for pleasantries? I shook her hand anyway. "Milly."

Laura opened her mouth to say something else, but was quickly interrupted as the giant, mahogany door we were locked behind began to open.

A small, studious-looking woman entered and silence fell. Her black hair was pulled into a tight knot on the top of her head, making the skin around her baggy eyes stretch past its limits. She held a few sheets of parchment in her aged hands.

"Hello, ladies," she chirped. "I am Lady Minerva."

No one responded.

Clearing her throat and adjusting her spectacles, she continued: "Some of you may have heard the rumors of the Princess's disappearance. The rumors are true, but King Leopold has decided to not let it discourage him. All of you young ladies have been chosen—"

"Chosen?!" someone shouted from among us. "More like taken!"

The woman rolled her eyes, annoyed by the interruption, and snapped her fingers. Two of the guards surrounding us snatched up the girl who made the outburst and rushed her out of the room.

"If any of you ladies cause anymore trouble, you will be severely punished."

We all jumped at the sound of a whip striking the poor girl in the hall and winced as her piercing screams reached our ears. Lady Minerva smirked at us.

"As I was saying, you were all chosen to be judged, and one of you will become the Princess's replacement."

We all gasped simultaneously.

You've got to be kidding me, I thought.

Minerva clapped her hands. "First thing's first! The King is going to choose which of you physically fits the criteria the most. Be respectful to His

Majesty and try to look pretty!"

I felt the blood leave my face. *King Leopold!* I thought. His reputation was not something to make light of. He was known as merciless and powerful, not just as King, but it was rumored he picked fights and killed just for sport.

The doors were pulled open again, but this time the King himself stepped through. He was a magnificent-looking man with shoulder-length blonde hair and a well-trimmed beard. His deep brown eyes stared each of us down with a terrifying intensity. A longsword swung back and forth at his hip as he walked, and his hand covered in many rings gripped the hilt of the weapon in what seemed to be a strange fondness. I gulped at the sight, my terror increasing tenfold.

"What number is this again?" he asked Minerva.

She curtsied to him. "This is the third group, Sire."

The King nodded. "There better be some more in this group. This is exhausting," he said.

Minerva paled. She bowed her head and stepped out of his way.

"Line up!" King Leopold bellowed.

All of us immediately scurried about to comply.

Rubbing his chin, he slowly walked down the line, vigorously shaking his head no at each girl he passed. I stood at the end of the line, shifting from foot to foot, not knowing what I wanted to happen. He nodded at the girl right before me, and she was led out of the room. He then stopped in front of me, and I froze.

"You there. Look at me," he said, calmer than I expected.

Forcing my body to stop shaking, I lifted my chin to meet his gaze. As I did so, my fear dissipated and the loathing I felt for our ruler took over. Who was he to take us by force and judge us like swine?

King Leopold raised an eyebrow in interest. "I want this one, too," he said, pointing at me.

I shook myself from his gaze. "What?" I tried to say, but nothing seemed to have come out.

I looked over my shoulder at Laura. Her eyes were wide, watching as I was hurried out of the room. That was the last I ever saw of her.

Chapter 7

I sat with five young women at a large, wooden table that stretched across the spacious dining room. Upon further inspection, I noticed one similarity among all of us: we each had long, blonde hair, like Princess Amelia. The shades varied, like mine was significantly lighter than the rest, but we were *all blonde*. They had dressed each of us in simple, yet uncomfortable gowns, probably trying to make us look more presentable. Mine was a very dull pink and was scratchy in all the wrong places. As if there were any *right* place to be itchy.

Ignoring my discomfort, I looked up and blinked in the bright candlelight as it shone within the elegant chandelier dangling above us. Surveying the rest of the room, I counted six intimidating guards. Borge, the one who had kidnapped me, was among them. All of us girls were too scared to speak, eyes wide in apprehension of whatever was to come. I kept thinking of Janice. She was going to be worried sick when I didn't show up, and all I wanted was to see her and be safe at home.

Footsteps sounded on the marble floor, and we turned. Lady Minerva was trotting toward us, same bored look on her pinched face as before.

"Good morning, ladies," she said, throwing a stack of books and papers on the table before us. "King Leopold has instructed me to start on your training."

Hands on hips, she surveyed the young women she had to work with. She didn't seem pleased.

Against everything in my gut telling me not to, I raised my hand.

Minerva turned her nose up at me. "Yes?"

I gulped. "Um, am I right to understand that you're training us to be the *actual* Princess?"

She rolled her eyes. "Mildred, is it?"

I nodded.

"We told you that when you first got here! You really need to pay attention. Another stupid question, and you will be whipped."

I almost objected, but I bit my tongue.

"Now, if there are no other questions, we will begin. First," Minerva spread the books across the table, "we read! Within these books and documents before you is everything you need to know as a princess: mannerisms, geography, politics... You get the idea. I will leave you ladies for the next eight hours, and I will expect all of you to have made significant progress. You will each be questioned right before dinner, so that we can evaluate your retention and learning abilities."

All of our mouths were hanging open as we

stared at the books and papers we were expected to read.

A girl beside me, maybe sixteen with beautiful brown eyes, slowly raised her shaking hand.

"What?" Minerva spat, exasperated.

"I can't read," the girl whispered.

Minerva rolled her eyes again, something she seemed very fond of, and snapped her fingers. One of the guards snatched up the poor girl and dragged her out of the room to... who knows where? Those of us left took the cue and scrambled to begin studying right away.

"Lunch will be brought to you in three hours. Don't stop studying, though!" Minerva shouted as she stepped out of the room. Two guards followed her, leaving three with us to supervise.

I looked down at the worn book in my hands. The title was hard to read due to the age of the book, but I was able to decipher the words, *A History in Politics of the Kingdom of Mardasia*. I groaned. Not only did it sound terribly boring, but it was, like, a thousand pages! But, out of fear for my well-being in this crazy situation, I got started. Who knew what would happen to me if I didn't cooperate?

Chapter 8

"Next!"

Wringing my hands, I stepped into the enormous library I had been in when I first arrived. Bookcases hugged the tall walls and so many candles burned in the room I was afraid the books would catch fire.

"Have a seat, Mildred." Minerva gestured to a cushioned seat across from her. She sat in front of a warm-looking fire, surrounded by her regular entourage of guards. The set-up was cozy... if you could disregard the circumstances.

"What did you read today, Mildred?" The light from the fire reflected off the glass of her spectacles, making it impossible to see the look in her eyes.

"Um..."

"You *never* start a sentence with 'um'!"

I clenched my fists in annoyance. "I read a lot of *A History in Politics of the Kingdom of Mardasia*, ma'am."

She raised a thin eyebrow. "Oh? That's all?" I really didn't like this woman.

"That thing was huge!" I gasped at my own outburst, and a couple of the closest guards started inching towards me, waiting for the command. Minerva waved them away.

"Fine. I'll just quiz you on some politics then. See how much you retained." She shuffled through a stack of papers on her lap. "Ah, here it is. Who was the first king of Mardasia?"

"King Geoffrey," I said without hesitation.

Minerva nodded. "What law was he most famous for?"

I knew this one, too. "Fathers were allowed to kill their daughters' lovers."

One of the guards snickered, and I chuckled back. It really was a funny law. King Geoffrey ordered it because his eldest daughter had a tendency for inviting male callers into her bedchamber on a regular basis. Minerva shot the guard a dirty look. He cleared his throat.

"That's correct," the woman said, flipping a page. "How many men are elected into the king's advisory council?"

I thought for a moment. "Ten," I said, confident.

Minerva slipped her spectacles down her nose and gave me a pointed look. "Eleven," she said.

I gulped. "That's right. I thought ten because our fifth king, King Bradley, had one of his advisors killed and was the only king to have ten during his reign."

"Humph," Minerva mumbled as she folded her arms across her lap. "I think we're done now. Joseph, please escort Mildred to dinner."

The guard to her right, the one who had laughed at King Geoffrey's law, nodded and gestured me to follow him out of the library.

"That's it?" I asked.

"I've heard all I need. For now."

So much for eight hours of reading, I thought, standing up and straightening my skirts. I then proceeded to follow Joseph out the library doors.

The halls were gloomy and lacked any real color. Each side of the halls were adorned with an abundance of paintings. Every royal depicted within the frames looked down at me with a regal arrogance. I couldn't help but admire each painter's ability to capture such a thing.

I looked ahead at my escort. He was tall with dark, wavy hair and walked stiffly, yet confidently. He didn't seem to be much older than I, and he *had* laughed during my meeting with Minerva. He probably wasn't so bad.

"Joseph?" I said, daring a conversation.

He stopped and turned towards me. "Yes?" He seemed shocked and confused by my speaking. He probably wasn't expecting to talk with a prisoner princess trainee, or whatever I was.

"Were you sitting in on any of the other girls'... tests, I guess you could call it?"

Joseph nodded. "Yes, miss." He turned on his foot and began walking again. I caught up to him and began walking by his side.

"How did I do?"

He shot me another confused look, but kept his rhythm in stride. "Better than some, I think, miss."

I chuckled. "Really? Mine was so short!"

I caught a little bit of smile on Joseph's face. He actually was quite handsome. "You were much braver than a couple of the girls. Two were so scared they couldn't even answer some of the questions."

I gasped. "What happened to them?"

He shrugged. "They didn't pass."

I stopped for a moment, causing him to halt. Something didn't feel right.

"What's wrong, miss?"

I hesitated for a moment, but feeling comfortable with him so far, I continued, "Where have they been taking the girls that fail?"

Joseph quickly lifted his finger to his lips, quieting me. He darted his eyes around the halls, looking to see if we were alone. He stepped towards me, our faces just an inch apart. I could feel his breath on my cheek.

"You need to be careful about what you're saying. I really shouldn't be answering your questions," he whispered. I quickly nodded, feeling scared all over again. He didn't move his face away from mine. He was close enough that I could count all the freckles on his face. I studied his deep, brown eyes, but couldn't find anything.

"Please, we have to hurry, or they'll suspect something." He started walking again.

I moved to follow, but was not satisfied. I was hoping to have gotten some more out of him.

Joseph led me to the dining hall the other girls and I had studied in previously, but this time the table was set with an abundance of food instead of a mountain of books. Even the *smell* of it was better than anything I've ever experienced. My mouth began to water. The fruit and cheese they gave me for lunch a few hours before had not been sufficient.

Two of the other girls were already sitting at the table, gazing at the food with eagerness. They were both very thin, and their gowns kept slipping off of their freckled shoulders.

"Was I last for the test?" I whispered to Joseph.

He gave me a curt nod as he pulled out a chair for me to sit.

Just three of us left, I thought. The contestants, if you could call us that, seemed to be dropping like flies.

As I sat, all the guards bowed their heads. The King had stepped over to the dining table. I sat up straighter, not knowing what to feel... whether it be anger, awe, or fright. I grabbed at my hands to stop from shaking.

King Leopold eyed each of us girls in turn for what seemed to be forever, then Minerva came waltzing in, first speaking in hushed tones to the

King. They each took seats at the table, King Leopold at the head, Minerva the seat next to his on the right.

"Ladies," Minerva said. "This dinner will be a lesson in table manners. First take the smallest fork to begin."

I looked down at the multitude of utensils in front of me. Why did there have to be so many? I could always eat everything with just one fork and, if need be, one spoon. Scratch that, all I *really* need are my hands.

As soon as my fingers touched the fork, four servants rushed in with plates and put a meager amount of the greens on the table in front of me. It was a small serving, especially considering how much was on the table, but I eagerly dug my fork into the salad.

"Mildred!" Minerva snapped.

I paused, food halfway to my mouth. What now?

King Leopold raised an eyebrow at me, and the other young women shot me nervous glances.

"Ladies, take the napkin at your place and set it across your lap," Minerva said, demonstrating with her own napkin.

We all followed suit, eager to start eating.

"You may begin," the King said.

My first bite of food finally made its journey to my mouth, and I trembled with satisfaction. It was the best salad I had ever had! With juicy chicken and savory cheese sprinkled all over it, and a sweet dressing to top it all off.

"Now, ladies. Be delicate! And sit up straight," the old lady barked.

I snapped out of my reverie and consciously made an effort to look poised. The girls beside me had trouble keeping their hands steady from nerves.

"Next course!" the King shouted, seemingly disgusted with his plate.

I had barely finished three bites before my plate was whisked away and a new one was set before me. A small serving of roasted potatoes, and a glowing piece of duck glistened on my plate. It smelled *divine*. If I hadn't been fearing for my life, this was something I could get used to. After we were directed to use the right utensils, I dug in. I tried to eat as much of it as I could while trying to look graceful at the same time.

"Dessert, please!" the King snapped, rubbing his belly. He was able to finish his whole plate. I watched sadly as a servant took the rest of my beautiful duck away. I couldn't have been eating it for more than thirty seconds!

A small cup of chocolate mousse met my eyes. I couldn't remember the last time I had chocolate. It didn't come by cheap.

Minerva lifted up a small spoon beside her dish and gestured for us to grab our own. Every bite of the rich dessert was heavenly, and, miraculously, the King took a longer time to finish this course than the others. He must have been savoring it, too.

I scraped at the final bits of chocolate on my dish with my spoon. The sound of the utensil clinked against the glass bowl loudly. Minerva cleared her throat, pointedly staring at me again. I set my spoon down and rested my hands on my lap, groaning inwardly.

"Ladies, as the King leaves the table, bow your heads in respect."

We did so as King Leopold pushed his chair back and briskly left the dining hall. He definitely wasn't there to socialize.

"Now, it is time to dance!" Minerva said, leaping from the table.

My stomach rumbled. I was still a bit hungry. Dancing didn't sound too appealing to me at that moment.

"You will each be paired with a guard in the room who will instruct you in the waltz. I will call in the musician to play the music!"

Joseph pulled my chair out for me and offered his hand. I took it, and he led me to the other side of the room, the dance floor I assumed. Two of the other guards in the room did the same for the other young women.

"You know how to dance?" I asked him.

"Of course! Even soldiers are noble. Though we are ranked lower than royalty, all nobles must know the ways of court— including dance. I've been to many balls and have danced with many ladies."

A short and plump man burst into the room and rushed to the grand piano in the corner, stern Minerva right on his heels. The pianist began playing a slow, pretty piece.

Joseph lifted my left hand onto his shoulder and placed his own on my waist.

"How much do you know about dancing?" he asked me.

"Enough to surprise you," I replied, winking.

Joseph smirked. "Let's just see how much you know. Follow my lead."

And follow I did. I was light on my feet, and he gracefully swept me across the floor. I could see the other girls struggling. They stepped on the toes of their partners, and one looked close to tears. My heart ached for them. I didn't know what to feel— a part of me wanted to survive the best way I could, and if that meant winning, so be it, but I didn't want those girls to fail, either.

"Where did you learn to dance like this?" Joseph said as he twirled me.

"My father loved to dance. He used to hold his own balls at home with my mother, sister, and me and would ask us each to dance with him." I smiled at the fond memory.

"Used to?" he whispered in my ear. Our faces were close.

"He and Mother aren't around anymore." I looked down at my feet, trying to hide my discomfort, but it made me stumble. Joseph caught me immediately and brought us back into our rhythm.

"I'm sorry. I shouldn't have asked," he said.

I shrugged. "It doesn't matter. Who knows if I'll ever get back home, anyway?"

He looked sad at that comment, but I brushed it off.

Out of the corner of my eye, I could see Minerva watching me, lips pursed.

"Does she have something against me?" I asked.

Joseph cast a quick glance at the woman. "Maybe, but I think her attention towards you has more to do with how well you've been doing in comparison with the other girls."

"Am I really doing that well?"

"In addition to your knack for dancing, you did far better in the test earlier than anyone else. I'm surprised the other two girls are still here."

That made me angry. This was all so unfair. "Do they really expect everybody to learn so much in just a day?"

Joseph looked around the room, wary. He lowered his voice even more than before. "They don't have much time."

"Time for what?"

He stopped leading me and studied me for a moment. I cocked my head and looked back at him, confused. He leaned forward, breath on my ear.

"I want to help you. Let's talk tonight. Don't look for me. I'll come to you."

The music came to an abrupt halt, and Minerva clapped her hands for everybody to stop dancing.

"Thank you, gentlemen!" she said. "And now it is time to retire!"

Chapter 9

My bedchamber was *huge*. Never had I seen such a large space for one person. It was at least twice the size of our single room cabin in Marviton! I had my own powder room with a beautiful, porcelain tub, a fireplace, and a mattress big enough for five people! The deep red wallpaper was gorgeous, and the rug spanning the room was just as soft as the bed. Under different circumstances, I would have felt like I was in heaven.

A maid had helped me dress out of that uncomfortable gown they put me in earlier and gave me a satin nightgown to wear, and I must say the nightgown was much preferred.

It was late, but I still sat in front of the unlit fireplace. I stared at the cold wood in the hearth, made visible by the moonlight shining through the room's window. The same thoughts ran through my head over and over again: Was my sister worried about me? What will become of me? But most of all, I was wondering about what information Joseph was going to give me tonight. Was he going to help me escape, even though that seemed highly unlikely? And where was he? What did he mean by "I will come to you?" Was he going to come to my room? I rubbed my temples with my fingers, head starting to pound.

A rap sounded at my door. I leapt up, startled. Hesitantly, I walked over to the door and pulled it open a crack. I saw Joseph peeking through at me.

"Mildred," he said. "I think everyone is asleep, but I can't come in. Leave the door cracked. I have to stay standing here, just in case someone comes by. You sit by the door."

"Okay," I replied, leaving the door open an inch and sliding to the floor. "Joseph, are you guarding my room?"

"Yes," he replied. "I requested it. I told Minerva you seemed like trouble, and that I wanted to keep a close eye on you."

I chuckled. "She bought that?"

I could hear the smile in his voice. "Yeah, she doesn't like you. She says you're impertinent."

"All I do is ask questions!" I huffed.

"All the same, I think you've been chosen."

"What?"

"Hush!" Joseph hissed. "We'll both be in a lot of trouble if they hear us."

I shook my head, frustratedly resting the back of my head against the wall. "They chose me? Already?"

"Like I said, they don't have much time."

"Seriously, Joseph! Time for what?"

"Look, I don't know much," he whispered through the crack, "but I do know that they wanted to have a new princess picked and trained by next week. There's something the Princess was supposed to do, but then she disappeared. No one knows *what* she was supposed to do. Well, except for the King."

"Why me?"

"You've done the best so far, and they need someone chosen *now*, so they can focus on one girl for the rest of the training."

I sighed. "I don't want to be the Princess."

We sat in silence for about two minutes. I had so many questions, but all I really wanted was to not be there.

"Joseph, aren't people going to wonder when they have a new Princess all of a sudden?"

"As far as the people will be concerned, the Princess will have never disappeared. Her being missing is just a rumor outside of the castle."

"But I don't look anything like her!"

"Mildred! Please keep your voice down."

"Milly," I said.

"Huh?"

"Please call me Milly."

"Milly," I could hear tenderness in his voice, "I really don't know the answers to everything." He paused for a moment. "You actually do have a bit of a resemblance to the Princess. You have the long, blonde hair, for one thing. Besides, I don't expect them to be parading you around everywhere."

"What about the girls who failed the testing?

What happened to them?"

He fell silent.

"Joseph?" I asked.

"Do you really want to know the answer to that question?"

His tone sounded dark.

Tears welled up in my eyes. "Laura and all those other girls…"

"Yes," he whispered.

I started sobbing. I felt sorry for all those girls, but ashamedly more sorry because I didn't know what was in store for myself. Joseph stepped into the room to sit next to me, ignoring what he had said earlier, and pulled me into an embrace. The hilt of the sword in his belt poked me in the ribs, but the hug was comforting all the same.

"I'm so scared," I croaked through my tears. He held me tighter. I felt his heart pounding against mine. Joseph intrigued me. I couldn't quite figure out why he was trying to help me.

"Milly, I'm going to be here for you in whatever way I can. I don't like what's going on, either."

"Then why are you here?" I said, pushing him away.

He frowned, furrowing his dark brow. "I want to make a difference. I dislike the tyranny just as much as anyone else."

Tyranny, I thought. I actually hadn't thought of King Leopold as tyrannical. Scary and a ridiculous spender, yes, but never tyrannical… Until he kidnapped me, that is.

"Why?" I asked, wiping away my tears. "Aren't you a noble?"

He nodded. "But that doesn't mean I like the way things are done. One day I'm going to be captain of the guard, and I'll make sure things change." His expression went dark. "No matter what I have to do, it'll change."

I leaned away from him against the edge of the door, starting to feel uncomfortable.

"Sorry," he said, playfully pushing my shoulder. "I can get intense sometimes."

I chuckled nervously. "What would you change?" I asked.

Joseph rested his forearms on his knees, interlocking his fingers. "Well, I wouldn't tax the people nearly as much. And I would help the less fortunate a lot more than they are helped now. I also think our judiciary system is highly flawed. I've seen so many innocent people killed just because the King said so." He clenched his jaw. "Like my father."

"I'm sorry," I said, touching his shoulder.

Joseph shook his head. "It was a long time ago."

"What happened?"

He looked down, shuffling his feet. "My father refused to kill a man who couldn't pay his taxes, so King Leopold had them both killed."

I gasped. "How terrible!"

"I want things to be different just as much as anyone, Milly," Joseph whispered, holding back tears.

I put my hand on his knee, hoping to comfort him.

Joseph smiled his charming smile. I blushed.

"I think we're going to be great friends, Milly," he said.

I nodded, trying to hide the reddening in my cheeks.

"Joseph," I said, "is it true that Princess Amelia ran away with a servant boy?"

He laughed unexpectedly. "Yes. And thank goodness they made it out, too! That boy would have been killed."

I hesitated before continuing, not sure if I could really trust Joseph, but the fact that he had just opened up to me was a good sign.

"I saw her," I whispered.

Joseph eyed me. "What?"

"The night she ran away. I let her buy my horse and helped her escape."

Joseph's eyes were wide, and his mouth hung open. "Are you serious?"

I nodded, and he started laughing again.

"What's so funny?" I urged.

"That's pretty ironic, don't you think?" he said.

I guess it is...

"I better get back out there." He stood up, then helped me to my feet. "I'm going to make sure you stay safe."

After shutting the door behind him, I tiptoed over to my bed and slipped into the covers. I gasped as the softness surrounded me. My bed at home was like a board compared to this! I slid myself deeper under the blanket and welcomed the warmth, but sleep was the furthest thing from my mind. I kept replaying the words, "I'm going to make sure you stay safe." I knew he meant more than just by standing outside my door. It was comforting to know that I had someone on my side.

Chapter 10

I stood with one other young woman on the palace grounds with a few guards as companions. The well-manicured lawns and the uniform trees were impressive. There were gardeners posted all around us tending to the landscape, and each time a colored, fall leaf blew off a tree, one of them rushed to catch it before it hit the ground. That seemed a bit unnecessary to me.

I glanced at the young woman beside me, and she caught my eye. She was smaller than me, but we were still roughly the same age. She seemed to be having a hard time breathing, and I wasn't much better off. We were both absolutely terrified. At the crack of dawn, we had been, for lack of a better word, *dragged* out of our beds and taken outside.

This must be the final test, I thought. *There are only two of us left.*

The air was chilly, but I couldn't tell if my body was trembling from the cold or from fear.

The sound of grass crunching behind us startled me, and I whirled around to find the source of the noise. Minerva briskly headed towards us,

Joseph close behind with a large target in his arms. Another guard, much smaller than Joseph in comparison, was on their heels with three bows and a sheath of arrows in hand. I raised an eyebrow. Bart had a bunch of different archery pieces at his store in Marviton, but I had never actually *tried* shooting a bow and arrow. I felt sick to my stomach and looked over to the other girl. She looked just as nervous, if not more than I was. She started biting her fingernails.

"Petunia!" Minerva shouted at the young woman. I had never actually heard any of the other girls' names until now. "Biting your fingernails is *not* princess-like!"

The poor girl's lip began to tremble as she threw her hands down at her side.

Minerva ordered Joseph to place the target a few yards ahead of us on the grass. As he went by, he gave me a quick smile. It helped calm me down a little bit. The other soldier with the bows and arrows placed them down in front of Petunia and me.

"Princesses are good at lots of things," Minerva said as she paced in front of us, "and one of the things that princesses are good at is archery." She gestured to the weapons at our feet. "In Mardasia, archery is a common sport and pastime for *all* noblewomen." Minerva squinted her beady eyes at us. "You can see why it is important that the Princess knows how to shoot a bow."

It seemed pointless to me, but I wasn't about to

argue.

"Pick up a longbow, each of you!"

We did so, and Minerva picked up the third one. She then proceeded to demonstrate how to hold the bow, place the arrow, draw back the string, and *twang*! She hit the bullseye on the first try. My jaw dropped to the floor. She made it look so easy. I stroked the elegant, smooth wood of the bow. She had called it a *long*bow. It was definitely long... I was afraid I wouldn't even be able to hold it up, considering how small my arms were.

"Petunia, you go first," Minerva said. She snapped her fingers and a guard rushed over to take the bow from her outstretched hand.

I could see her throat move as Petunia gulped. We all stepped out of her way as she took position. She struggled to place the arrow just as Minerva had. It kept slipping out of her grip, and she didn't even get to pulling the string back before Minerva got impatient.

"Good heavens, child!" she said. "You have the coordination of a blind man with no thumbs!"

I had to bite my tongue to stop myself from shouting at the woman. How dare she expect us to be perfect princesses within a week?

"Mildred, you go," Minerva snapped at me.

Pressing the bow tightly against her chest, Petunia backed away, trying to hide the tears that spilled down her rosy cheeks. I felt my heart grow heavy for her, understanding completely how she felt.

I stepped slightly forward and took a deep breath. I lifted the bow to position, struggling against the weight. I reached into the sheath of arrows as Minerva and Petunia had and pulled one out. Placing the arrow wasn't the hard part for me, it was trying to draw the string back. My arm shook from the strain, and I found myself grunting as I tried to pull it back to my cheek. Without warning, the string snapped and hit my left arm. I cried out from the pain, dropping the bow and holding my arm as tears stung my eyes.

Minerva sighed. "I have so much work to do. Someone take Petunia away. Both were terrible, but Mildred was better, even if by a little."

I gasped as two soldiers ran out of formation and hooked Petunia's arms into their hands. She didn't scream, she didn't cry. She just bowed her head sadly, seemingly accepting her fate. Completely forgetting the pain in my arm, I watched in horror as they dragged Petunia through the grass and towards the castle. I couldn't feel happy for being chosen—I just felt guilty.

"Joseph, lead Princess Amelia back to her room. She has a long few days ahead of her."

Did she just call me Princess Amelia?

Joseph saluted to Minerva, jaw clenched. I couldn't read his expression. Minerva left just as fast as she had come, and the rest of the soldiers followed her back into the castle, leaving Joseph and me alone.

All of the pent-up anger I had been pushing

away for the last few days came boiling up inside of me. I turned to Joseph, fuming.

"How could you let this happen? How could you let them just *take* her like that?" I charged at him and pushed at his shoulders. He didn't budge.

"Milly," he whispered, grabbing my arms and holding me still. "We can't talk here."

He jerked his head to the gardeners surrounding us. Each of them stood watching me, shocked from the outburst. They all knew I wasn't the real Princess, but my anger was still surprising to them. I wanted to scream, but I relaxed my body and let Joseph direct me back to my bedchambers.

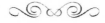

It had been *hours* since Joseph had taken me to my bedchamber. I was alone, pacing from end to end of the room nonstop. Joseph told me to stay calm right after the archery test and locked me in from the outside. Is this how it was going to be? *Be* the new Princess, but always stay locked away like a prisoner? I threw myself onto my mattress and screamed into one of the million pillows on the bed. A part of me would have almost preferred to be dragged off and killed like the other girls.

I perked up as I heard the doorknob to my room jiggle. Someone was unlocking it. I looked out my bedroom window, studying the darkness outside. It had to be close to midnight. No one had come in to give me orders, food… nothing.

"Milly?" Joseph said as he pushed the door open slightly. The one candle burning on my nightstand came close to blowing out from the air in the hallway.

I sat up in bed, arms folded. I was still wearing the gown a maid had dressed me in this morning, so I could barely see Joseph over the mountain of dark, green skirts surrounding me. I glared at him, saying nothing. He craned his head back to see if anyone was near us outside, then, satisfied, tiptoed into my room, leaving the door open just a crack.

"There was nothing I could do, Milly. You have to understand that." He stood at the foot of my bed, hands clasped in front of him. He seemed tense and kept his eyes at his feet.

I swung my bare feet over the mattress and jumped off, which was quite a feat, considering how far it was from the ground. I made my way over to the window and stared out over the castle grounds. They were illuminated by the moon, it being large and yellow that night. I stared at it, wondering how far away it was and how I could get to it: to just keep going towards the moon and never stop…

"I hate it here," I whispered.

Joseph hesitated, but then inched towards me. I flinched as his hand touched my shoulder, but I didn't push it away. Earlier, I wanted nothing to do with him, but in that moment, I desperately needed a friend. I turned to him, tears welling up in my eyes.

"Joseph," I said, "Why me? How am I supposed to live like this?" I threw myself against his chest and sobbed into his uniform. The wooly material scratched against my cheek, but I didn't care. I welcomed the warmth of his arms as he wrapped them around me. He stayed silent, but I knew that he felt sorry for me.

Chapter 11

The next few days were excruciating. As the chosen "Princess," I had hours upon hours of training to do. Reading, horseback riding, archery (which I was actually getting better at), more reading... It was endless! But every night I got to talk with Joseph. After a tiring day of work, I always had that to look forward to. But I was going through an *especially* tiring day. Minerva had me read a few hours' worth of books, and then I spent a few hours with the tailor to size me for a plethora of gowns and dresses. How much clothing did one girl need?

"Knock, knock," Minerva said, bursting through my bedroom door. "How are the fittings coming along?"

"They could be better," the stingy tailor said.

"Oh?" Minerva eyed me disapprovingly.

"I didn't do anything!" I gasped at my own outburst, expecting Minerva to punish me. She just eyed me, seemingly annoyed.

The tailor put his hands on his hips and flipped his blond bangs out of his face. "She is so *skinny*! It' sickly! I have to take in all the Princess's dresses.

Do you know how hard that is?"

I set my jaw and clenched my fists. This little man was so *irritating*, but I was afraid of what might happen if I spoke up again.

Minerva clicked her tongue. "Lord Plum, do as you're told! And she *is* the Princess! You will refer to her as Princess Amelia."

He grumbled.

"Oh, heavens!" Minerva cried, clutching her chest. "The things I have to deal with around here! Maid!"

My maid, yes, *my* maid, was sitting in the corner. She leapt up as she was beckoned. "Yes, m'lady?"

"Kindly dress Princess Amelia."

The maid curtsied.

"And Princess?"

I looked at the woman, trying not to make my distaste of the entire situation seem too obvious.

"Kindly report to the library in half an hour. You have a lesson on tea time."

"I need a lesson on tea time?"

Minerva pursed her thin lips and glared at me. "Of course you do."

I groaned inwardly. All I wanted was a little sleep.

Minerva and Lord Plum stepped out of the room so I could start changing.

"What would you like to wear, Princess?" The maid stepped over to the enormous, mahogany wardrobe in the room. The heavy-set girl struggled as she tried to pull the doors open.

"Patty?" I said to the maid.

"Your Highness?" She curtsied.

"Will you please just call me Milly?"

She shook her head, brown curls bouncing out of the kerchief tied around her head.

"Even if we're in private?"

"I could get in big trouble, m'lady," Patty said. She looked frightened.

"Fine," I said. "And about what to wear, just pick something for me. I really don't care."

Chapter 12

"Tea time always happens in the afternoon in between lunch and dinner, and there is a correct etiquette that all nobles are expected to know."

I rested my face in the palm of my hand, eyes growing heavy as I listened to Minerva drone on about the only thing I ever heard: etiquette, manners, nobles…

"Princess, elbow off the table!"

I slid my elbow off the small tea table Minerva and I sat at. From the corner of the library, I heard Joseph, who was appointed to guard us during this lesson, snicker at me. I flashed an annoyed look at him, but he winked at me. I found myself smiling at the gesture. Minerva didn't notice as she surveyed the setting before us.

"To your left are the sandwiches and scones."

I looked to where she pointed and saw a mountain of delicate, tiny sandwiches and some glowing pastries— the scones, probably. I still wasn't used to the type of food the nobles had available to them.

"Why are there so many for just the two of us?"

Minerva rolled her eyes and gracefully picked a

sandwich off of the platter and indicated for me to do the same. The soft bread squished between my fingers, and I did everything I could to not let its contents drip all over me, or the pretty lace cloth set over the table. I took a bite and grimaced. It was just cucumber. There was no flavor and over-all just bland.

Joseph made a knowing face behind Minerva's back, and I chuckled.

"What is so amusing, Amelia?" Minerva seemed to relish in the taste of her tiny sandwiches. She would, though.

I cleared my throat. "Nothing, Lady Minerva. I'm sorry."

She raised an eyebrow at me, but brushed it off and instructed me towards the scones. Those were significantly better, and still warm. As I fin-ished my pastries, Minerva lifted up one of the smaller tea set pieces. The glass was ornately dec-orated with intricate blue paintings of flowers.

"This is the creamer," she said to me. "Milk is poured into the teacups before the tea— always!"

I couldn't understand why she always had to snap at me.

Minerva poured some milk into the delicate teacup before me, then followed with some pip-ing hot tea.

"Sugar?"

I nodded.

She gingerly placed two cubes in my cup and directed me to stir with the tiny spoon next to me. I slipped the silver utensil between my fingers and stirred the liquid in circles. The spoon clinked against the glass, and Joseph grimaced at me. I raised an eyebrow at him as he chuckled slightly and shook his head.

"Amelia!" Minerva gasped. "Do *not* hit your spoon against the sides of your cup! And *never* stir in circles." She picked up her own spoon and stirred her drink back and forth in small movements— much less effective, in my opinion.

Minerva proceeded to list about a hundred more rules for tea time, and I groaned inwardly as my head started to hurt. It was ridiculous to have so many "correct ways" to do things. It accentuated the loss I felt as I thought of home and its glorious simplicity.

After we had finished with the tea, Minerva set the napkin from her lap back on the table. I followed suit.

"Dinner is in two hours, Princess," she said as she rang a bell to call a servant in for clean-up. "I will send a few more books to your room that I expect you to start reading while you wait."

I glanced at Joseph, and he shrugged. He knew how much I had read in those past few days. It never ended.

"Joseph." Minerva pushed her seat back and stood, turning to face him. "Will you take the Princess back to her room?"

He nodded his head and gestured for me to follow him.

"And one more thing, Princess."

I whirled around to acknowledge Minerva.

A little smile appeared on her cracked lips as she continued: "You will be addressing the court and the King in the throne room tomorrow morning. Be on your best behavior."

"I—I—"

"Don't stutter, Amelia. Princesses do *not* stutter."

I bit my tongue. I was shocked. I had to address the King? What for? Well, I guess I was his "daughter." I couldn't help but keep thinking about what his plan was— About why he chose to replace the real Princess.

Joseph and I remained silent as we strolled down the hallways, in fear of someone overhearing us. Joseph had told me a couple days ago that it wouldn't bode well if people knew of our friendship. We reached our bedchamber, and he pulled my door open.

"I'll see you tonight," he whispered.

He gave me another wonderful smile, but my mind was still on what Minerva had said to me.

The King had not been at dinner that night, as per usual. I actually hadn't seen him in days, which made this "addressing the King" event even more scary to think about.

I let Patty pull the gown off my head and stared at my bed. I would have just gone straight to sleep if it wasn't for how excited I was to talk with Joseph. After Patty left, I waited by my bedroom door, eagerly awaiting his knock. I waited for at least a half an hour before it came.

I cracked open the door.

"Milly?" he said.

I sighed with relief. "You have no idea how good it is to hear someone call me by my real name."

"Can I come in?" he asked.

"Are you sure it's safe?" I said, pulling the door open wider.

"I won't stay in for long. I just like talking to you face to face."

I smiled. "Me too."

He wrapped me up in a warm hug. I closed my eyes, breathing him in. He smelled like grass and trees, which kind of reminded of home.

"Oh, Milly," he said, grabbing my face.

"Uh, yes?"

Joseph chuckled and let go of me. "I'm sorry. I just really enjoy our little talks. And I got a little worried."

"Worried?" I asked, sitting down on the floor. He followed suit.

"You're addressing the court tomorrow."

"Well, I am the 'Princess' now."

He nodded. "I know, it's just... it's an intimidating thing to have to see the King in such a formal setting."

"What do you mean?"

"Everybody from the court will be there. All the noblemen and women, and the castle servants, know you're not the real Princess, so they'll be watching everything you do. Not to mention that addressing the court and King so formally always warrants some sort of announcement."

I cocked my head. "Announcement?

He stroked his chin, deep in thought. "Maybe you'll figure out what it is the Princess was supposed to do."

I sighed, exasperated. "I'm so tired, Joseph. I miss my sister. I miss my home."

He scooted over to me and put his arm around my shoulders. "I know."

Footsteps sounded close to my chamber. We both perked up. Was someone listening to us? My heart jumped to my throat. Thinking about being caught made me want to throw up.

"I'll be right back," Joseph said, jumping up to get to his post again. He quietly shut the door behind him.

I wrung my hands, nervous, as I waited for what seemed to be forever.

The door opened again, and he slid through.

"I made it out in time," he said. "It was just a guard making his rounds. I think he was drunk, too." He took his seat next to me and put his arm around me again.

"Phew," I said, chuckling.

"Milly, can I ask you something?"

"Sure."

"If things were different, do you think... you and I...?"

I paused, not sure what he was trying to get at. We had been getting rather close lately, but I didn't think anything could ever come of it.

Joseph brushed off what he said. "Never mind. I just wish things were different, especially for your sake." He frowned and started picking at the soft, red carpet we sat on.

I turned my face to his and smiled. "Hey, *you're* the one who's supposed to do the comforting."

He laughed. "I know. My job is to save princesses."

I nudged him. "Stop," I said, also laughing.

"I love your laugh," he said.

I blushed, turning away. All of this flirting was not something I was used to. I didn't interact with many boys my age back in Marviton.

"I'd better get back out there," Joseph said. He looked a little embarrassed by my silent response to his compliment. "I'll see you tomorrow."

I watched as he stood up and slipped back out the door. I sighed, feeling bad for making him feel uncomfortable. As I moved to get into bed, my thoughts kept going back to Joseph, and I found myself grinning. I thought of his crooked smile, and the way his dark hair curled around his ears. My face grew hot, and I shook my head. How would anything like that ever work? I was the Princess now, and it wasn't like I was going to escape anytime soon. And he was a royal soldier! He wouldn't run off with me... would he? I groaned and threw the covers over my head, telling myself to stop thinking about it.

Chapter 13

"Do I really need to wear this? It's so cumbersome!" I choked past the ruffles of the neck to my dress.

My maid Patty and Lady Minerva were both helping me dress to visit the King. My hair and makeup had already been done by the royal hairdresser. I almost screamed when I had looked in the mirror and saw a giant tower of blonde curls on my head and blotches of red on my cheeks and lips.

"Princess," Minerva said, "it is important to wear the appropriate attire to court. This gown is regal and befitting royalty."

I groaned. "I feel like I can't move." I pushed away all the blue fluff to try and find my feet.

"Maid, please assist Her Highness into her shoes."

Patty gestured for me to sit in a chair and helped slide atrociously green heels onto my feet. At least they matched the dress.

"You are ready!" Minerva cried, clapping her hands. "This is so exciting! Your first time in court! I heard the King has a special announcement!"

"Um, Lady Minerva, everybody knows that I'm not Princess Amelia, right?"

"Hush!" Minerva snapped at me. "You *are* Princess Amelia."

I took a deep breath. "Okay…"

"And please, for heaven's sake, speak like a princess! Don't let all of that training go to waste!"

I stood up straighter. "Yes, Lady Minerva."

"Off we go!" Minerva chirped, leading me out of the room. Patty curtsied and was left to straighten up the mess we made while getting me ready.

I followed Lady Minerva down the long hallway towards the throne room. My palms were sweating. I didn't know what to expect out of this visit with the King, let alone a bunch of nobles!

We finally made it to the tall doors. With a nod from Minerva, the two guards stationed pulled them open.

"I will go in first and introduce you. You're on your own after that," she muttered to me under her breath.

I gulped.

Minerva stepped into the spacious room, shoes clicking on the granite floor. "The Princess Amelia."

Taking a deep breath, I made my entrance. A couple dozen nobles surrounding each side and King Leopold lounged in his throne at the head of the room. Trying to control my shaking, I curtsied. Out of the corner of my eye, I saw Joseph standing among the nobles. He gave me a thumbs up, and I felt myself gain a little more confidence.

"Princess Amelia, my daughter, how have you been? Have whatever ailments indisposing you been healed?" the King said. His voice was loud enough to be heard in the entire room, yet he sounded gentle. But his eyes were dark with no emotion.

I hesitated at his question of my being sick, but then remembered everybody in the room knew I wasn't the real Princess. This fabricated story — for the sake of the people outside the castle— would be that I was just indisposed for a time.

"Yes, Sire. I feel much better now," I said.

He nodded. "That is wonderful news."

I curtsied yet again, and he gestured for me to take the smaller seat to the left of his. As gracefully as I could in my heels, I made it to the plush chair and sat down. My heart was pounding so fast that I felt like it was going to jump out of my chest.

King Leopold stood to address everybody in the room. "Now that my daughter has graced us with her presence, I am excited to announce an event that you have all been eager to hear, I am sure."

If the room wasn't quiet before, it definitely was now.

"Queen Andromeda from the Polart Kingdom and I have come to an arrangement." King Leopold grabbed my hand. I shivered.

"Her son Prince Alexander and my daughter Princess Amelia are engaged to be married, which will thusly join our kingdoms in a beneficial arrangement for all of us."

My jaw dropped, and everybody in the room gasped. It was silent for a short moment, but then excited chatter began. My jaw was still hanging open.

The King clapped his hands for silence. "Yes, this is a joyous event! I invite you all to a feast tonight in honor of this arrangement and in honor of our Princess Amelia!"

I searched for Joseph again. He looked red in the face, fists clenched.

Married? I thought. *To a prince I've never met? What kind of messed up joke was this?* But then again, why was I surprised by anything at this point?

The King turned towards me. "Congratulations, daughter." Then lowering his voice so no one else could hear, "You will be a great help to me."

Chapter 14

I sat next to the King at the head of the large dining table. Each chair was filled with a noble, and each noble was dressed in vibrant colors and made up in extravagant ways. There was not one face at the table that didn't have at least a touch of rouge painted onto their cheeks. All eyes were on me during the feast. I knew they were judging every move I made, just waiting for me to slip up. I wasn't going to give them that satisfaction. With every course, I made sure to eat with delicacy, and I spoke with poise and even a hint of pomp. I was engaged in conversation during the whole dinner, barely getting in more than just a few bites of the delicious food. You'd think a princess wouldn't be as hungry as I always seemed to be.

"Princess?" an older man said a few seats to the right of me.

I gently dabbed at my mouth with a napkin and turned to him. "Yes, Lord…?"

"Chamberlain," he said, grinning.

My stomach turned as I watched the powder on his face crack as he smiled. "Lord Chamberlain?"

"How do you feel about your engagement?"

I looked to the King out of the corner of my eye, but he made no reaction as he scooped bite after bite of his soup into his mouth.

I tried to think of the best answer to satisfy the man. "I feel as elated as any woman might be in the situation, my Lord."

The man winked at me. "I hear Prince Alexander is quite the catch. Rumor has it he has broken many ladies' hearts in his day."

"That's... good to hear," I said, forcing a smile. I caught Joseph's eye from across the room where he was stationed. His eyes did not leave me. His brows were furrowed, and his lips were pursed into a tight line. I could tell he wanted to talk to me. The feeling was mutual.

"That's not what I heard!" someone chimed in.

I turned my head to see who the voice belonged to. A young noblewoman with very bright, green eyeshadow winked at me. She continued:

"Prince Alexander is very handsome, but I heard he is cripplingly shy."

I raised an eyebrow, trying to decide what was better: a heartbreaker, or a recluse.

"Next course," the King bellowed.

Everybody dropped their soup spoons at once and waited for the next plate to be served. Quickly set before me was a beautiful chicken breast lying in a pool of gravy. I waited for King Leopold to take a bite, and then I got to it. I ate as quickly as a well-mannered princess could muster.

Dessert came in and went just as quickly as the other courses, and before I knew it, the King called for the dancing to begin. I sighed with relief.

This is my chance to talk with Joseph, I thought.

Lord Chamberlain leaped from his seat as soon as the musicians began playing music and rushed over to help me out of my chair.

"Your Highness," he said. "May I have the honor to dance with you first?"

"Of course," I said, hiding the shock from how fast he was to get to me with that ancient body of his.

Taking his hand, we made our way to the dance floor. The dress I was wearing for the celebration was much better than the blue monster earlier. I felt satisfied with my ability to walk as I watched the light-weight, pink layers swish across the floor.

Lord Chamberlain faced me and bowed. I curtsied back, and we started dancing. A lot of the other guests followed our example and began dancing, as well.

The Lord pulled me so close as we danced that I could smell the moth balls in his wig.

"You know, Princess," the stench of alcohol on his breath burned my eyes, "you are much prettier than the real Princess."

My eyes widened, surprised by the statement. "Lord, you are not supposed to mention her. I *am* Princess Amelia, remember?" I looked around the room, nervous someone would hear our conversation.

Lord Chamberlain licked his lips. It was a grotesque sight. "We all know that you're not Princess Amelia, my dear. For you, being with a Lord like me should be an honor."

He tightened his grip around my waist. It took everything in me not to slap the stupid grin off his face.

"My Lord," I said, thinking quickly, "I'm feeling rather faint. Will you help me to a chair?" I gestured toward some chairs set along the wall at the end of the room, near where Joseph was standing.

The Lord raised an eyebrow, dropping his hands off of me. "Of course, Your Highness."

I accepted his outstretched arm and allowed him to escort me. I sat down on a cushioned chair and smiled at the Lord in thanks. He bowed his head, looking disappointed and left to find another young lady to torment. Joseph slowly started inching towards me.

"Milly," he whispered. He kept his eyes on the dancers.

"Are you not allowed to be dancing?" I asked.

"I'm on duty," he replied. "But *you* should be dancing, not talking with me. People will get suspicious if you're just sitting chatting with a guard all night."

"Humph," I said. "That Lord Chamberlain was a snake."

Joseph looked disgusted. "I know."

"Am I interrupting something?" A young nobleman stepped to us, looking at Joseph curiously.

"No, sir," Joseph replied, standing at attention. "Her Highness was not feeling well. I was asking if I could be of assistance."

"Oh?" the young man said. "I was coming to ask the Princess for a dance. If she is feeling unwell—"

"No, my lord. I am fine to dance. I just needed to sit a spell."

"In that case." He offered his arm. I shot Joseph an apologetic look, but he kept his eyes on the party.

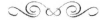

I must have danced with twenty men that night, all with varying, yet extreme, personalities. Most of these noblemen, as far as I could tell, had one thing in common: they loved hearing themselves talk. The noblewomen weren't much better. Most of them conversed with me only out of obligation, but it didn't stop them from turning their noses up at me and whispering behind my back.

I finally found a seat and tried to rest my legs when the King approached me and bowed his head.

"Daughter," he said, "may I have the last dance of the evening?"

My mouth went dry, but I somehow found the words, "Yes, Sire."

His arm was stiff when I took it, and he escorted me to the center of the floor. Everyone watched us in interest. They would probably just say they were happy to see the King dance with his daughter, but I couldn't help but think it was more like excited to see the King dance with his *new* daughter.

"You dance very well," the King said as we stepped to the music.

"Thank you, Sire," I said, though I felt like I was shaking too much to dance as well as I was normally capable.

"The arrangement with the Kingdom of Polart is a very good one, Amelia."

I merely nodded. The King could kill me at any minute if I said the wrong thing.

"I'm sure you're excited to meet your future husband."

I searched the King's eyes, but still found nothing. He was very good at hiding his thoughts.

"Of course, Your Majesty."

We danced in silence for about a minute. No one else was dancing, they were just watching. It was as if everyone around us were holding their breath. I knew *I* was. It took that minute for me to muster up the courage to continue the conversation.

"Sire," I said, "when will I meet the Prince?"

"Two days time," he said without hesitation.

I choked. "So soon?"

King Leopold raised an eyebrow at me. "The sooner the better."

The song ended, and he bowed. I curtsied in turn and watched as he briskly left the floor. I felt sick to my stomach. Things were happening so fast. I stumbled, but Lady Minerva caught me quickly. I hadn't even noticed her at the party all night. I was so caught up in everything else.

"Is she alright?" I heard a few voices shout out in the crowd.

"Just fatigued," Minerva called out, assuring all the worried nobles. "She has been dancing all night. Am I correct in saying so, Princess?" She gave me a look that dared me to say otherwise.

"She is right," I said. "I would very much like to retire."

The crowd parted to make a pathway for Lady Minerva and me. I nodded politely to all I passed. A few gave me sympathetic glances, but most were just curious as they tried to get a good look at me.

After making it out of the dining hall, I pulled away from Minerva's grip.

"I think I can manage on my own," I said to her.

"Fine," she said, "but I'll walk you to your room."

Just as we were about to head for my bedchamber, Joseph stepped out of the dining hall.

"Oh, good," Minerva said. "Your guard is here. Will you escort the Princess back to her chambers? I would like to rejoin the party."

"Yes, my Lady," Joseph said.

Minerva left quickly. I had never seen her so excited. She must really like parties.

"What luck," I said, smiling at him. He smiled back, but he looked a little tense.

"Let's start walking," he said. "We have to be careful what we say. There are a lot of people around."

I nodded.

"Milly," he whispered, walking close to me, "I didn't know about the engagement. I would've warned you."

"I know," I whispered back. "It's not your fault."

He clenched his jaw. "Why would the King make you do this? He's got to have a selfish reason."

I thought for a moment. "I do know that our kingdom and theirs don't always get along... And the Polart Kingdom *is* very wealthy. Are we having any financial issues?"

Joseph shrugged. "If we were, there is no way *I'd* know about it."

We made it to my room, and Joseph opened the door for me.

"We can't talk anymore right now with the party still happening," he whispered to me. "I'll talk to you later tonight, though. I think I have an idea."

"Really? What idea could you possibly have?"

Joseph held his finger to his lips. "I hear someone coming. I'll talk to you soon." He shut the door after me.

"Your Highness?"

I whirled around to see the maid Patty standing right behind me with a feather duster.

"Is everything alright?" she asked.

I grabbed my chest. "You startled me!"

Patty shifted her blue eyes to the floor. "Sorry, Your Highness."

I put my hand on her shoulder. "It's alright. Can you please leave me alone, though? I have had a long day."

She curtsied, gathered her skirts, and slipped out the door. I saw Joseph give me a concerned look before the door shut again. I was thinking the same thing. I really hoped she didn't hear any of what we had said.

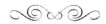

Having left the loud party early, King Leopold lounged peacefully in his chair, satisfied with the events of the day. His plan was underway, and the new Princess wasn't causing any problems as of yet. She was doing a lot better than he anticipated, and she looked the part rather decently. Overall, it was like Amelia had never left. He could care less about where his actual daughter was, or what she was doing.

Leopold picked up a book he was in the middle of and contentedly started reading. He suddenly heard a knock on his study door. *What now?* he thought, setting his book down.

"Enter," he sighed.

A guard poked his large, square head around the door. "Sire?"

"What is it?"

"The Princess's maid has requested an audience with you. She says it is urgent."

"Really?" Curious, King Leopold sat up straighter in his chair. "Let her come in."

A larger young woman shuffled into the room, not much older than sixteen. She curtsied.

"Forgive me, Sire, for disturbing your privacy."

He lifted his hand to silence her. "Please get to the point quickly."

The girl gulped, wringing her hands together to control her shaking. "I wanted to come straight to you. I think the Princess and her, um… guard are getting a little friendly."

"Oh?" the King said, rising from his chair. "What is your name, child?"

"Patty, Your Majesty."

He stepped closer to the young woman. "I assume you must know what happened to the last maid that served the Princess Amelia."

She nodded quickly, paling. "Of course, Sire. That's why I came right to you."

He smiled at her. "I'm very glad the woman's fate inspired you." He stood directly in front of the maid, hands behind his back. "Now, please elaborate on the situation."

"I've only just seen looks, Sire. And not half an hour ago, I heard him say he had an idea."

The King rubbed his beard. "An idea for what?"

Patty looked at her feet. "I don't know, my Lord."

King Leopold slowly walked back to his desk. "My dear, that is hardly evidence for anything."

The girl shuffled her feet. "I'm sorry, Sire."

He sat down. "Don't be. It is good to be cautious. And now I have a job for you." He gestured for her to come closer and lowering his voice said, "I need you to spy on them for me, just to be safe."

The girl winced, seemingly reluctant.

Leopold sighed. "You will be greatly rewarded."

She perked up and nodded. "Yes, Sire. Thank you, Sire"

"Who is the guard?" the King asked, mindlessly drawing circles on the desk with his finger.

"Joseph, my Lord."

Leopold chuckled. "Ah, Lionel's son," he said, thinking of the guard he killed all those years ago. Such a good soldier... What a waste. "Does he guard her at night?"

"Yes."

"Go now," he said. "I wonder if they talk to each other when everyone's asleep."

The maid curtsied and hustled out of the room at his dismissal.

King Leopold picked up his book again, smiling.

He wasn't going to let anything get past him this time.

Chapter 15

I recognized Joseph's knock anywhere. I eagerly cracked the door open and let him slide in. He pulled me into a tight embrace, and I found myself melting into his arms.

"Milly," he said after we pulled apart, "we're going to get out of here."

"What?" I cried. Joseph threw his hand over my mouth. He had said the words I had been *dreaming* to hear for the last two weeks, but how was it even possible?

"That's our only option," he whispered, slowly taking his hand away.

I shook my head. "How?"

Joseph quickly looked through the crack in the door to make sure no one was coming.

"There's got to be a way," he said. "The Princess did it. The chamber I sleep in is close to the ground. I bet we could crawl through the window and get out of here."

"You sleep?" I chuckled.

He playfully nudged me. "Usually during the day. I'm always on duty at night, as you know. Anyway, no one would expect the Princess to be in that area of the castle."

I shook my head. "It sounds too easy."

"We'll give you a servant's disguise," he said, getting excited. "If anyone sees us, it'll just look like a guard sneaking around with a maid, which isn't unheard of in this castle."

I was getting excited, too. The idea of getting out of this situation was very appealing. "Do you really think this will work?"

"I do," he said. "But we'll need to get provisions and means of travel outside of town."

"I actually don't think we need to worry about that. We can travel to my home in Marviton— my sister can probably help us."

He grinned and proceeded to bounce up and down a little. I laughed at his enthusiasm.

"I'll need time to find a maid's dress for you, and then we can leave tomorrow night," he said.

We heard a rustling outside the door, and we both started. Joseph went back into position, and I shut the door.

I listened nervously and heard Joseph talking with someone. My door opened, and I leapt back, shocked. It was Patty.

"Your Highness, I just wanted to check on you. I was coming this way, and I heard talking."

I tried to think quickly on my feet. "Um... well, the guard..."

Joseph stepped into the room, too. "I heard the Princess screaming, and I burst into the room to make sure she was alright. Turned out she was just having a nightmare."

Patty nodded. "Of course. That makes sense. I'm sorry to bother you, Princess."

I shot Joseph a grateful glance. "It's quite alright, Patty. Thank you for your concern."

She curtsied. "If that'll be all, Princess?"

I dismissed her, and she left.

"That was close," I breathed out, relieved.

Joseph squinted his eyes in suspicion. "I'm not entirely sure she was just 'walking by this way,' Milly."

"What do you mean?"

"When I came out of the room, she jumped away from me as if she was listening at the door."

"What?" I said, not wanting to believe it.

"We need to move," Joseph said. "Now."

"Should we get her?" I asked, suddenly terrified. I grabbed at my heart, chest tightening.

"No," Joseph said, grabbing my arm. "She'll just scream. We need to get out of here quickly. I give it five minutes before she alerts the King."

I let Joseph drag me out of the room, and we ran down the hall together. My breathing was hard, and I tried not to shout out from his pulling my arm so hard.

"My bedchamber is one flight down," he said to me. "We can make it before she gets to the King. If we're lucky, she's taking her time. She might think that we don't know she was listening."

The stone stairs were cold on my bare feet as we hurried down them. Joseph constantly looked behind his shoulder, each time running a bit faster.

Miraculously, we ran into no one as we made our way into Joseph's bedchamber. It was much smaller than mine with just a tiny bed and a chamber pot. The wallpaper was a boring gray, and the floor was stone instead of carpet, but that made sense, considering our ranks were so far apart. Joseph let go of my arm and pried open the window next to his bed. I watched, trembling as the cold air from outside hit me.

"Joseph," I said, "I'm only in a nightgown."

He turned to me, frowning. "I didn't even think about that. Quickly, go to my closet and try to put on some of my clothes. Put on some socks, too. It's better than nothing."

I nodded, rushing over to the closet and throwing on a thick, red tunic over my satin nightgown. I wasn't even going to *try* to put on some pants—they'd slide right off of me.

"Milly, it's a little bit of a jump. Let me go first, then I'll try to help you out next."

I moved over to the window and watched as Joseph threw both legs over the sill and leapt out. His feet landed with a thud.

"Come on, Milly," he said to me, sweat dripping on his face. "It's your turn."

The way to the ground was maybe ten feet. It wasn't too bad, but it still made me a little nervous.

"Hurry!" Joseph called, desperate. "They'll be after us any minute now."

I flipped my right leg over then followed with my left. "You'd better catch me," I said.

I jumped, and he caught me with ease.

"Run!" he said, grabbing my hand.

And run I did. The dew from the grass soaked the socks on my feet, causing my toes to go numb, but I didn't care. We were getting out of there.

King Leopold watched out his study window as his new Princess and that young guard ran off the grounds. He ran his fingers through his hair, contemplating his next steps.

"Are you sure you don't want us to go after them?" a guard with the name of Borge asked.

The King looked over to Borge, grinning. "I want them followed, but not too far. Don't catch them just yet. This maid tells me they're headed for the sister." He nodded towards Patty huddled in the corner of the room. She bowed her head, avoiding eye contact.

Borge saluted. "Yes, Sire."

"Report back to me as soon as you find out which direction they are headed. Then I will give further instruction," the King said as he casually moved to sit back in his chair.

Borge grunted in agreement and left the room.

King Leopold clasped his hands atop his desk. "Thank you, maid. You were very helpful tonight."

A tear dropped off the young woman's nose and onto the carpet.

"Why are you crying?" King Leopold said, irritated. "You did the right thing."

"What will happen to them?" Patty whispered.

He raised an eyebrow at her. "If I were you, I wouldn't be asking any insufferable questions."

She nodded, lip trembling.

"Now leave me."

Patty curtsied and shuffled out as quickly as she could.

King Leopold sighed in relief. "Alone at last," he muttered, pulling his book out again.

Chapter 16

"Joseph," I said.

Joseph stopped for a moment to look at me. "Are you okay?"

My legs began to wobble as I stood still. "No," I said. "My feet."

His eyes shifted to my cold feet, only covered with the thin, wool socks I had thrown on before we left.

"The rocks on the road... they're digging into my feet." I said, shaking. The cold was piercing my skin like little daggers.

He nodded. "It's gotta be uncomfortable."

I chuckled, despite myself. "That's an understatement."

"We need to find a horse, anyway. We can't make it all the way to your sister's without one — not before they catch up to us." Joseph warily looked around. We were at the very north edge of Capthar, about a mile away from the castle. Just a few houses surrounded us, having not entered the main city yet. "Actually, I'm surprised they *haven't* caught up to us."

"Joseph!" I said, suddenly remembering.

"There's an inn in town, not far from the square. I left my horse there before I was brought to the castle!"

He grimaced. "That's dangerous," he said. "We really should stay on the back roads."

"There won't be anywhere to find a horse on the backroads," I said.

"You're right," he said. "Here, I'll carry you a little ways. I think I know what inn you're talking about." Joseph swept me off the ground and started sprinting again before I could say anything.

I felt the muscles in his arms pulse against my body as he ran, then blushed as I caught myself thinking too much about his muscles. I rested my head on his shoulder, grateful for the break on my feet.

"It's actually faster this way. Even with you carrying me, we're going faster than me trying to run with you," I said.

Joseph laughed through his heavy breathing. "It's not easier, though."

"Are you calling me fat?" I teased.

"Never," he replied, chuckling.

We stayed silent for a few minutes, which gave me the chance to really think about what was happening. I couldn't believe we made it out of the castle at all. But the farther we got away, the more nervous I became that I would be taken again. I searched the tall trees in the woods next to us, hoping nothing would jump out of the shadows.

"I'll put you down when we get close to the inn. If people see us, I don't want them asking if you're hurt and try to help us. We need to move quickly."

I looked up at his face, noticing his flushed cheeks and the sweat on his brow.

"Do you need me to walk now?"

He shook his head. "I can go a while longer." He started running even faster.

"Are we getting pretty close?" I asked a few minutes later after Joseph gently set me on my feet again. We had made it to a more densely populated street. There were more shops and homes on each side of us. Though no candles were lit in any of the windows, suggesting people were asleep, we still tried to avoid standing in the light of the streetlamps.

"Yeah," he said. "If we turn right here, we can cut through some alleys and make it to that inn you were talking about in just a couple minutes."

We both jumped at the sound of the bushes next to us rustling and laughed nervously as we saw a rabbit hopping out of them.

"Come on," he said.

I followed him off the road and toward the center of town and recognized the alleyways as the route Borge and Jared took Laura and me through not long ago. I shivered, convinced it would happen again.

"Is that it?" Joseph asked, pointing ahead.

I squinted my eyes through the darkness to see what he was pointing at. "Yes!" I said.

"Let's hurry!"

We crossed the street, and I was quickly able to tell that Borden and my wagon weren't at the post I had tied them to, understandably. It had been more than two weeks since I'd paid that stable boy to watch over them.

"I'm sure my horse is in the stable," I said quietly.

We tiptoed over to the modest stable, careful not to draw attention to ourselves.

"Hopefully everyone's asleep," Joseph said. "This is the largest inn in town. There are probably a lot of people staying."

I looked towards the building and did not see any candles flickering in any of the windows. That was a good sign.

As we approached the horses, we saw the young stable boy keeping watch, sitting on a stool in front. He was playfully burning a piece of hay in his candle's flame.

"Hey, it's you!" he said to me, leaping up with a grin on his face. "You're dressed... differently."

I looked down at my outfit, socks on my feet with my shins bare and a men's tunic hanging past my knees.

"I've seen weirder, though!" the boy exclaimed. Joseph and I quickly shushed him.

"Oh, right," he chuckled. "Folks are asleep right now." His freckled nose crinkled as he gave us a huge smile.

I smiled back. "Do you still have my horse?"

"Sure do, ma'am." He tried to brush the hay off his shirt. "But I didn't think you'd ever come back! It's been days!"

I held my finger up to my lips again.

"I'm sorry. I've always had such a loud voice." The boy hit himself in the head playfully. "I took the liberty of locking up your horse, ma'am. Just in case you ever did come back." He gestured for us to follow him.

"I really appreciate it." I looked to see about ten horses on each side of me. Most were asleep, and the rest were too tired to make much noise.

"Hey, did you hear that the Princess running away was just a rumor?" the boy said as he led us to Borden's gate.

Joseph and I shared nervous glances.

"Yeah, apparently she was just really sick. I don't know how that silly rumor started up in the first place! But I hear that she won't be making any appearances any time soon, not that they do much of that, anyway. Always having parties to attend." His bright green eyes looked into the distance dreamily. "I've always wanted to go to a royal party." The young man opened the gate and patted my horse on the nose. Borden whinnied happily, obviously familiar with the stable boy. "Do you want me to get your wagon? It's in the back. The innkeeper was adamant on getting rid of it, but I convinced him to hold onto it a little longer."

"If I let you sell it, do you think you can get some money out of it?" I asked him, patting Borden on the nose myself.

The boy's eyes widened. "Yes, ma'am! I think I could!"

"Keep it then. In return, do you have a spare saddle?"

He nodded. "I'll be right back, ma'am!" The boy scurried off.

Joseph stepped over to the horse and gently stroked his pelt. "What's his name?"

"Borden."

"Beautiful horse," Joseph said to me.

The stable boy ran back to us. He looked even smaller than before as he tried to lug the saddle over. Joseph hurried to help him throw it over Borden's back.

"Thank you, sir!" the boy said enthusiastically.

Joseph helped me onto the horse's back, but before he took a seat behind me, he slowly looked over his shoulder.

The stable boy cocked his head, looking in the same direction as Joseph.

"What is it?" I asked, hands beginning to shake.

Joseph's hand rested on the hilt of his sword, and the seconds we sat in silence felt like minutes.

"I thought I saw someone..." he said. Shaking his head, he relaxed and leapt behind me onto Borden.

"Um..." the stable boy muttered. He was still looking out into the night. "Travel safely," he said, seeming confused.

"Thank you so much, boy," Joseph said to him.

The boy shook out of his thoughts and looked back to us. "My name's Charlie, sir. Glad to be of service!"

"Thank you, Charlie. You've been awfully sweet." I gave him a big smile.

Charlie blushed. "Anytime, ma'am."

Joseph kicked the horse, and we were off. With his arms reaching around me, Joseph used Borden's dark mane to guide us onto the road.

"Do you know your way home using the back roads?" Joseph asked me as we trotted away from Charlie. The boy was energetically waving good-bye.

"Yes," I said. "I often went that way because the scenery is so much prettier than on the main road. It does take a half a day longer than the normal route, though."

"It's our best bet. We don't want to be travelling where a lot of other potential travellers will see us." Joseph clicked his heels again, bringing Borden to a faster pace and soon turned him left at the fork, heading for the back roads.

"Once you get to the back road, just keep heading south," I said to him.

I felt his chin bounce on my shoulder as he nodded.

"Did you really see someone back there?" I asked nervously.

He didn't answer, but then said, "I can't help but think our escape was too easy."

He was right: our escape really *was* too easy.

It was hard not to think the worst. We rode in silence and trotted at a decent pace, but not fast enough whereas Borden would get tired too quickly.

After a few minutes, Joseph perked up and looked over his shoulder.

"No!" he hissed.

"What?" I said, trying to swivel my head around.

"Don't look," he said. "Someone's following on another horse. They're not too far behind."

My heart started pounding, and I could hear the blood rushing in my ears.

"What do we do?"

"We have to try and lose 'em." Joseph dug his heels into Borden's flank, and the horse bolted.

I craned my neck to try and see our pursuer.

"He's struggling with his horse!" I said.

Joseph turned to look, still keeping Borden at a steady sprint. The person following us was having a hard time getting his horse to match our pace. The figure was falling more and more behind with every second.

"Let me know when you can't see them anymore. I'll make some random turns once we're out of view!" he shouted over the wind.

I kept my eyes on the distant horseman, watching as he turned into a black dot.

"I don't see him anymore!"

"Good job, Borden!" Joseph praised the horse. "Milly, I can't see so well in the dark. Are there any turns coming up ahead?"

I squinted, looking into the distance. "Yes! Right turn!"

"I see it now!" He prepped Borden.

I held on tightly as Borden turned, trying not to fall off. I didn't know my horse was so fast!

Joseph took a few more turns after that, keeping Borden at the same pace. The wind stung my eyes, and the cold bit at my unprotected legs. After a good amount of time, Joseph slowed the horse to a steady trot.

"I don't want to get him tired," Joseph said.

I crouched down and patted Borden's flank appreciatively.

"He's a great horse," Joseph said to me.

I kept looking over my shoulder, nervous. "Do you think we really lost him?"

"I think so," he said. "Do you know where to go from here?"

"I've never been on this road," I replied.

He seemed thoughtful. "Maybe if we just start traveling south again for a while... We'll figure it out."

"The sooner we get there, the better." I said. Seeing my sister sounded so appealing, but I knew we had to get as far away as possible, and quickly.

King Leopold sat in front of the large fireplace in his bedchamber and watched as the embers crackled and formed various shapes. He was confident his new princess wouldn't get away like his daughter did. They caught word of escape much sooner than last time. Although, he *was* perturbed by the irony of the situation. Both ran off with a stupid beau. Amelia had claimed she was "in love" with that servant before she disappeared. Leopold had laughed at her, claiming how ridiculous love was. He still felt that way.

Someone knocked.

"Enter," he bellowed.

The burly guard Borge rushed into the room, Minerva right on his tail. Both bowed their heads.

"Well?" King Leopold demanded.

"Sire, I followed them for a good half an hour before they caught sight of me," Borge said.

"They saw you?" He didn't shout, but the King's words hinted at irritation.

Borge shifted his eyes to the floor. "With all due respect, my Lord, we were the only ones on the road. They were bound to see me at some point."

King Leopold rolled his eyes. "Do you at least know where they were headed?"

The guard nodded, enthusiastic. "They were heading south on the backroads. I even heard the Princess *say* to head in that direction."

Minerva shuffled forward with a large piece of parchment rolled up in her arms. "If I may, Sire?"

Leopold gestured at the small table in his room. Minerva unrolled the parchment, revealing a map of the kingdom. The King rose from his chair and leaned over her shoulder. He and Borge watched as Minerva traced her finger along the backroads of the map southward.

"There are only two small towns that align with that path, my Lord," Minerva said. She looked up at the King, eyes gleaming under her spectacles. "Pouthose and Marviton."

The King grinned, moving back to his warm chair. "Borge, assemble two teams to investigate both villages. Ask around. If you find the sister, you find her. Move out *now*."

Borge saluted and ran out of the chamber. His shouted orders to the other guards pierced the silent halls and through the King's walls.

"Minerva," Leopold said. She stood up straighter. "Prepare the Princess's things. She will be leaving for the Polart kingdom as planned, and on schedule."

She nodded, quickly gathering the large map in her arms and shuffled out, closing the door behind her.

The King laid further back in his chair, sighing. He turned his attention to a full goblet of wine he had left on the short table next to his chair and pulled it into his grasp. He gulped it down in seconds and began humming to himself, watching the flames in the fireplace again.

Chapter 17

We were able to find our way back onto the right road quickly and traveled a good distance through the night. Borden had taken us maybe forty miles within just a few hours, with us only stopping a few minutes at a time for Borden's sake. It normally took me about a day with my wagon to travel *thirty* miles.

"We need to let Borden rest for a couple of hours," Joseph shouted to me over the wind.

I studied the sky. The stars had started to disappear a little bit, indicating that it was maybe two or three hours before dawn.

"Okay," I said, yawning.

"I'm tired, too. Maybe we can find somewhere hidden to sleep for a little bit." He pulled on the reins and slowed the horse down to a steady trot.

I glanced behind my shoulder for probably the thousandth time, almost expecting to see someone following us.

"How far are we from Marviton?" Joseph asked as he studied the dark trees for somewhere safe to rest.

"I think we're probably twenty or so miles

away." I couldn't stop from worrying about being caught as I kept my eyes on the dirt road.

"There," Joseph said.

I looked to where he pointed. To the left of us was a patch of very tall grass that led into a small opening behind some large pine trees.

"There seems to be room to hide Borden behind those trees, and we can sleep in the grass," he whispered.

Joseph turned Borden in the direction of the nook. It was very dark behind the trees, but that was a good thing. The better hidden we were, the safer I felt.

Joseph jumped off of Borden and outstretched his hands to help me down. Touching my feet to the grass reminded me of how wet my socks were. The blades reached up to my knees and scratched uncomfortably against my bare skin.

"I'm freezing," I said as Joseph tied Borden's reins to a strong-looking tree branch. My teeth chattered uncontrollably.

Joseph looked at me sympathetically. "We'll need to stay by each other for warmth." He paused. "Of course, if that's okay with you."

My cheeks started burning at the thought of being so close to him.

"Yeah..." I replied.

Joseph walked over to where I was standing and laid down on the ground. I hesitated, but then followed suit. The grass began to rustle as he scooted closer to me, then wrapped his arms around my waist. He was so warm. The back of my head was pressed against his chest, and I could almost hear his heart pounding— it was fast. I held my hands tightly against my sides, not sure what to do with them.

"Does this help?" His breath tickled my ear.

"Yes."

We were silent, the sound of crickets the only thing reaching our ears. I kept thinking about how close I was to Joseph, and how nice it felt.

"Milly, what is it like in Marviton?"

I was surprised by the question. "Um, it's very small. Everybody knows each other. Janice, my sister, and I live on a little farm in our cabin. Father built it when he and Mother were first married 23 years ago."

"You lived there your whole life?"

I nodded. There was another minute of silence before he continued:

"How did your mother die?"

The memory shot a pang through my heart, and my head started to hurt. I always tried to avoid thinking about that night three years ago.

"Uh..." I croaked.

"We don't have to talk about it. I'm sorry," Joseph said, voice softening.

I shook my head. "No, it's okay. It's good to talk about it, I think. Father... he was always drunk, and it drove my mother mad. She got to the point where she couldn't get out of bed anymore, and then one day, she just... died."

"Oh. Milly, I—"

"Don't," I said. "It's okay. Father left right after. I thought he hated me, and it took me years not to blame myself, but it's in the past." I clenched my teeth and tried to turn my heart cold to the memory. "Janice never really recovered."

Joseph tightened his arms around my waist to comfort me.

"I lost my mother, too."

I craned my neck to look at him, hearing the tears in his voice.

"How?"

"She got sick soon after my father was killed. No one really knew what ailed her, but my father's death had broken her heart."

I turned to face him and looked into his teary eyes. "I'm so sorry."

He laughed at himself, removing an arm from my waist and wiping his tears away.

"I'm not usually this open with anyone," he said.

I smiled. "I like it."

We looked into each other's eyes for a moment. The little light from the moon peeking through the trees above us glinted against the brown in his eyes, making them seem lighter than they normally were. He lifted his hand and began stroking my cheek. I held my breath, relishing in his touch as it sent shivers down my spine.

I moved away as I felt my cheeks grow uncomfortably hot and pressed my face against his chest.

I found myself breathing in his pleasant, woodsy smell.

Joseph stroked my long hair with his hand. "You should sleep."

"What about you?" I said through a big yawn.

"I'll let you sleep for an hour first. Someone needs to stay awake. Just in case."

I grimaced. I had almost forgotten about the danger we were in.

"I'll sleep after you," he said. "But we'll need to get back on the road soon."

I nodded, nestling deeper into his warm body. Regardless of the circumstances, I felt safe wrapped in his warm arms and fell right to sleep.

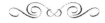

It was nearly midnight the next day as I banged on the door of the cabin I had grown up in. The chill air didn't bother me as I stood eagerly waiting for Janice to open the door.

"Is she even home?" Joseph asked after we waited for what felt like a second too long.

"She's probably sleeping," I replied. "And the door's locked, otherwise I would just walk in."

At that moment we heard some shuffling on the other side and the door unlatching. Janice's face peeked through the crack she opened in order to see who it was. Her green eyes widened and tears began to spill out of them.

"Milly!" she cried, flinging the door open.

Tears of my own joined her sobs as we held each other tightly.

"Milly," Joseph whispered, looking over his shoulder. "We should go inside."

I nodded and gently pushed Janice back into the cabin.

"Um, where should I tie Borden?" Joseph said, still holding the horse's reins.

"There's a post in the back," I said, waving him away.

Janice grabbed my face in her hands. "What happened to you?"

I shook my head. "First, I need to sit down. Do you have anything to eat?"

"Of course," Janice said, rushing into the kitchen.

I practically fell into one of the wooden chairs around our dining table. I stroked the table, chuckling. Our cabin was quite different from the elegance of the castle. It was comforting to look about and see the simplicity again. The small stone fireplace, the splintering wooden floor, the creaky ceiling... It was old and falling apart, but no elegance or luxury could replace *home*.

A soft knock sounded on the back door. I rushed to unlock and open it to let Joseph in. His boots creaked on the floor as he moved past me, surveying the space.

"We need to re-lock all the doors and cover the

windows," he said.

Janice swept back into the room right as we were finished securing the doors and windows. In her hands was a plate full of bread, cheese, and fruit. It wasn't as extravagant as the castle food, but I was grateful. Finding my seat again, I dug my hands into the food and stuffed my face. It felt *so* good to not worry about being polite! Joseph stepped over to a chair next to me and followed suit.

Janice sat across from us and watched for a couple minutes as we shoveled food before she cleared her throat. We sheepishly looked up at her.

"Milly, what on earth happened to you? And who's this?" She darted her eyes nervously in Joseph's direction.

Joseph leapt out of his chair, realizing his rudeness. "The name's Joseph," he said, bowing his head, and reached out his hand. "And you must be Janice."

Janice raised an eyebrow. "Um, yeah." She took his outstretched hand in hers and shook it.

I wiped strawberry juice from my mouth. "Janice, you'll never believe what I've been through."

I started from the beginning, only stopping to answer her questions. Mid-through the story, her tears returned, and she proceeded to shake her head in unbelief.

As soon as I was done explaining, she rose from her chair and knelt beside mine. She grabbed my hands in hers and said, "What do you we need to do to get you out of here?"

"We've been here too long already," Joseph said, moving to peek through a covered window by the front door.

I nodded. "We need supplies."

Janice gave me a look up and down. "And some new clothes."

"Milly?"

Janice and I looked towards Joseph, who was still looking out the window.

"We need to hide. Now!"

"What?!" I cried, rushing to the window with Janice at my heels. A group of soldiers dressed in the royal red and blue were just a few meters away from our position. They were conversing with various passersby and knocking on doors. I felt like I was going to faint.

"Father's stash!" Janice hissed.

"Of course!" I said, grabbing Joseph and dragging him over to my bed in the corner.

"Stash?" he said. "What does that mean?"

"Just help us move the bed," I snapped back. "Quickly!"

We each grabbed a corner and moved the bed aside, revealing a dusty rug. I hurriedly pulled that aside and saw the trap door for the first time in a long while. Without question, Joseph peeled it open and peeked into the hole.

"I can't see much," he said. "Will it fit us both?"

"Yes," I said, pushing him in and following right

behind. The space was barely large enough to hold us both lying down, nearly on top of each other. Joseph wrapped his arms around my waist and pulled me tight against his body. We looked up at Janice, who knelt at the opening.

"I'll close it up and move everything back over it," she said, getting up and brushing off her skirts. "I'll come get you when they're gone."

And at that the trap door was shut over us, making it pitch black. The dark didn't normally bother me, but being in this tight space where mice might be crawling around made it a bit scarier. My heart pounded in my chest, and I could feel my palms sweating.

"Too long in here, and we won't be able to breathe," Joseph whispered. His mouth was right next to my ear. I could feel him shaking from fear. I'd never really seen him so scared.

"How did they find us?"

I felt his head shake against my shoulders. "I don't know."

We fell silent for a minute or two, trying to listen to what was happening.

"I don't hear anything," I said.

"They probably haven't gotten to this house yet."

I felt myself begin to tremble and Joseph held me tighter.

"What did you and your sister mean by your 'Father's stash?'" he whispered.

I grimaced at the memory. "Since Father was an

alcoholic, he *always* had supply on hand," I said. "He kept it all in this space to hide it from my mother. Janice and I threw it out after he left us."

"I'm so sorry," he said.

The faint sound of the door opening and muffled voices sounded.

"They're here," I hissed.

Joseph and I went completely still, fearing to speak or even breathe. We felt the vibration of footsteps above us as the soldiers searched the cabin. I could hear Janice asking them what was going on, and the rough voices of the guards in return. I couldn't hear much, but I did hear bits and pieces.

"Do you have a sister?" a familiar-sounding voice said to Janice.

"Yes, sir," she replied.

"Do you know where she is?"

I gasped, realizing the voice belonged to Borge, the guard who had kidnapped Laura and me more than a week ago, getting me into this situation in the first place.

"I haven't seen her for days, sir."

I grinned, proud of how convincing she sounded.

"You will let us know if you see her?"

"Is something wrong?" Janice asked him.

"Just checking in on some things, miss."

Their footsteps faded away, and I couldn't hear the rest of their conversation.

We waited anxiously for what seemed to be an

eternity before Janice pried open the door above us. We blinked at the harsh light as we climbed out.

"I waited ten minutes after they left, just to be safe," Janice said.

Joseph nodded. "Let's gather all the supplies we can. We'll wait to load the horse until nightfall. We need to make sure they are far from town."

Chapter 18

After waiting a couple hours, we were convinced the soldiers had left Marviton. We still had four or five hours of darkness left, which made it a good time to start travelling without drawing too much attention to ourselves.

I was helping Joseph tie some of the food to Borden's saddle and trying not to cry again. Janice tiptoed outside with the last bit of supplies we had gathered and handed them to Joseph.

"That's all the jerky we have left," Janice said.

I bit my lip. "Will you come with us?"

She shook her head. "Three can't fit on one horse. I'll just slow you two down."

We pulled each other into a tight hug. "I'll be back someday, I promise," I said, burying my nose into her shoulder. It was too much. First I lost my parents and now my sister.

Janice stroked my hair. I had never seen her so brave. It was almost as if she was beginning to take on the role of elder sister.

"Home will always be here," she said. "*I* will always be here."

"Did you hear that?" Joseph whispered.

My sister and I released each other, each with our ears perked. Before I could even blink, half a dozen men leaped from the bushes and trees surrounding where we stood. Janice and I screamed and Joseph drew the sword at his hip. But before he could fight, he was grabbed from behind and restrained by one of the soldiers.

"Jose—" My shout was muffled by a hand thrust over my mouth. I began squirming, trying to get a good look at my captor. It was Borge! I tried to scream through his hand, my worst fears being recognized as I was being grabbed twice by the same man in such a short time. I bit down on his palm, hard.

"Wow! You're a feisty one, aren't ya, Princess?" His deep voice rumbled unpleasantly. My struggling only tightened his grip on me.

Darting my eyes around, I could see Janice and Joseph struggling with their own captors. The remaining men surrounded us, swords pointed threateningly.

"Men, grab your horses!" Borge shouted, which caused my ears to ring painfully.

And before I knew it, all three of us were tied and thrown onto horses. My life was, yet again, being ripped away from me after less than a day of freedom. I let myself cry. My shoulders heaved from the sobs. I didn't care who heard, I didn't care who listened. It was over.

Janice, Joseph, and I knelt before King Leopold in his throne room. It was very late, and the room was lit only by two candlesticks set on each side of the King's throne. The four of us and three other guards were the only ones present. It was a very different atmosphere than when I had last been there to address the court as Princess Amelia.

My wrists were chafing under the ropes that bound me. Out of the corner of my eye, I could see Joseph twisting his hands against his own ropes furiously. Janice, on the other side of me, looked up to the King, white as a sheet. Her entire body was shaking.

"Princess Amelia, your actions are... disappointing." The King's voice, though calm, carried loudly in the spacious room. I refused to look in his eyes, biting my lip so hard that it bled.

"And you," he said, turning his eyes to Joseph. "How dare you defy your oaths to the crown. You have committed high treason against your King, not to mention your kingdom."

Joseph clenched his jaw and shot a fiery glare at King Leopold.

The King shook his head. "Joseph Farthing, you are sentenced to an immediate execution."

"No!" I shouted.

King Leopold rested his eyes on my face, and

for a moment, I thought I saw a flicker of amusement in his stormy eyes. He snapped his fingers. One of the guards in the room drew his sword and approached Joseph, face stoic and unforthcoming. I began to squirm violently, but another guard came up from behind and held me still.

The guard with the sword grabbed a tuft of Joseph's hair and yanked his head back, revealing his white neck.

"I sincerely hoped that you wouldn't have the same fate as your father, boy. But I guess you're just as much a traitor and coward as he was," the King said.

Joseph clenched his fists and tried to leap out of the guard's grip. "*You're* the coward!" he spat. "My father was better than you will *ever* be!"

King Leopold didn't even flinch at his words. He nodded at the guard and in one fleeting moment, I watched as Joseph's throat was slit open. I stared, horrified, as the red blood dripped down his front and stained his clothes. The guard let go of Joseph's head and his body slumped, lifeless, to the floor.

"No!" I screamed. "How could you?!" I fought the man holding me back, trying to reach Joseph's body. Janice began crying hysterically beside me.

King Leopold snapped his fingers and another soldier immediately grabbed Janice by the arms and dragged her across the floor and out the door. Her screams echoed from the hall outside.

"No! Please no!" I begged. My tears were hot and

my voice was growing hoarse. "Where are you taking her?"

King Leopold leaned forward in his chair and smiled at me, his eyes lighting up with pleasure. "Princess Amelia, you will cooperate from now on, or your dear sister will be like Joseph there." He waved to the corpse right next to me.

My lip trembled, and I felt the blood leave my face.

"You will leave for the Kingdom of Polart tomorrow morning, as originally planned." He leaned back in his chair, seemingly exhausted. "You are dismissed."

Chapter 19

I rode in the royal carriage on my way to the Polart Kingdom, feeling completely numb, yet horribly nauseous at the same time. I replayed Joseph's death over and over again, clenching my fists tighter every time. I wanted to die. That was way better than the alternative.

"Princess?"

I didn't even look up at Lady Minerva sitting across from me in the carriage. She lounged comfortably on the red cushions with a blanket wrapped around her shoulders. It was still early in the morning, though we had already been travelling for two hours. She had been napping the bulk of the trip so far.

"You look ill, Princess. Do we need to take a break?"

I didn't answer and shifted my eyes to the window, staring blankly at the raindrops trickling on the glass.

Minerva sighed. "Bad things happen to the people that deserve them, Amelia."

"Stop calling me Amelia!" I snapped.

The woman raised a penciled, black eyebrow at

me. "You will be grateful to know that I will let that one slide, Princess."

I turned my attention back to the window, thinking of my sister. She was the only reason I was still going along with this nonsense.

"How much do you know about the Polart Kingdom, Princess?"

I shrugged, still refusing to make eye contact with her.

Minerva sighed again, moving her glasses a bit to rub at her temples. "I'm just going to keep talking and assume that you are listening."

I ran my finger along the cold glass of the window, welcoming the cold and adding it to the numbness I felt.

"The Polart Kingdom is known for its farming industry, whereas we are bigger in metal exports, which you should already know from your training. The Polart Kingdom's economy is almost always stable, which will be beneficial for our kingdom with your union to Prince Alexander. Not to mention the peace it will bring. The Kingdoms of Polart and Mardasia have been at the brink of war against one another many times. Boundary disagreements, I believe. Also, you should know, the death of their king ten years ago is a very delicate topic. I wouldn't mention that at all."

Minerva kept talking for the next hour or so, but I was only half listening. I already knew most of the stuff she was talking about from my "princess" training earlier, or from things I already knew. My gaze never left the outside of the window. I watched as we passed one rolling green hill after another. The rain had stopped, allowing a ray or two of sunshine to peek out from the clouds.

"We're reaching the borders of Polart," Minerva said excitedly, joining my watch out the window. "The castle isn't too far from here, actually. It's located very close to the edge of their land."

Within those next ten minutes, we entered a large town, about the same size as our capital. I craned my neck a little and was able to see the large castle not too far from us. It was made of magnificent white stone and towered much higher than ours. I found myself gaping at the sight.

Along each side of our carriage, people stared curiously at us passing by. Many of them pointed and excitedly followed us a little ways. The town was very similar to Capthar with merchants, inns, restaurants, and people busying about on their various schedules.

But there was one thing in particular that caught my eye: I squinted out the window and saw a very old, ragged woman with twisted gray hairs sticking out in patches on her scalp. She stood in front of a makeshift tent and shook a tambourine while she danced barefoot atop the cobblestones of the street. Something about her seemed so familiar. She seemed to be shouting something, but the glass made it so I couldn't hear. Most people seemed to be ignoring her.

Minerva glanced at me and tried to look towards what I was staring at.

"Witches," she muttered.

"What?" I said, thinking back to what Bart had said all those days ago when he showed me the *Book of Magic* at his store. He couldn't have been right, though. Could he?

Minerva shivered. "I heard the rumors, but hoped we wouldn't see any of it."

"What?" I pressed.

Minerva made eye contact with me, and I felt wary at how pale her face was.

"Sorcery," she said. It's been spreading a lot in the other kingdoms, especially Polart. If my suspicions are correct, that woman performs dark magic."

My stomach turned, and I kept my eyes glued on the strange woman as we passed her. For a brief moment, the woman caught my eye and grinned her rotted smile at me. I felt a strange sense of violation and quickly turned my gaze to the inside of the carriage.

"Disgusting," Minerva said.

But there was something more than that... It was like the woman had looked straight into my soul and knew who I was. Where had I seen her before?

Within the next ten minutes we reached the palace grounds, and the castle was even more impressive up close. Squinting against the sunlight, it looked as if specks of gold sparkled inside the marble stone of the structure, and the grounds were maybe twice the size of ours. Hundreds of soldiers dressed in the dark reds and purples of Polart marched along the cobblestones, protecting every inch of the area.

As we approached the front doors, servants began to pile out and line the entrance in order to greet me. At the end of the line came who I could only assume was the Queen and her son Prince Alexander. There was a stark difference between the two— Queen Andromeda stood regally at the entrance, sharp nose held in the air and red lips pursed into a strong, thin line. But the Prince shuffled his feet about, constantly straightening the thin frames of his spectacles and smoothing the mess of blond hair on his head.

"He is so handsome!" Minerva exclaimed, hands clutching her chest.

I snorted, but then my mind went straight to Joseph again. I clenched my jaw and tried to push down all the despair and anger.

We pulled to a stop, and our footman hurriedly leapt from his seat at the front of our carriage and pulled open our door. Taking his outstretched hand, I gingerly stepped out onto the ground in my heels. It was *really* hard to keep a pleasant look on my face. I wasn't looking forward to this at *all*. Minerva followed right behind me, helping push some of my skirts out of the carriage.

I raised my eyes to the Queen and the Prince and curtsied. The Queen nodded her head in acknowledgment, and the Prince avoided my gaze completely.

"Welcome to the Kingdom of Polart, Princess Amelia." Queen Andromeda's voice was low and sultry, yet powerful. Looking into her eyes, I almost saw displeasure as she looked me up and down. "This is my son, Prince Alexander." He bowed to me.

"It's a pleasure to be here, Your Majesty, Your Highness," I said. "It's beautiful here."

She dismissed my compliment and quickly turned her back to walk inside. Her long, raven locks bounced elegantly as she stepped away. The Prince gave me a quick smile then followed suit.

"Um..." I whispered.

"Follow them," Minerva hissed to me, giving me a little push.

As I passed each of the servants, they bowed and curtsied. They chattered excitedly to each other as I crossed the threshold of the castle.

The interior took my breath away. In front of me was a grand staircase made of a beautiful, pink ivory wood, and the handrails were encased in gold. Above me was the largest chandelier I had ever seen, decorated with too many diamonds to count.

"Princess," the Queen's voice echoed all the way to my ears, though she was all the way across the spacious entryway. "This is Clara," she said, gesturing to a scrawny maid at the foot of the staircase. She couldn't have been more than fourteen and must've seen labor every day of her life. "She will lead you to your bedchamber. I suggest you freshen up quickly. Dinner is within the hour."

With that, she turned on her heel and walked away again, Prince Alexander following her like a lost puppy. It took everything I had in me not to roll my eyes.

They really *know how to welcome a guest*, I thought.

Clara curtsied to me. "If you will follow me, Princess."

My shoes clicked on the marble floor. It was so shiny that I feared it would shatter under my every step. Minerva's eyes bulged out of her head as she stood surveying the entryway.

"Lady Minerva," I said, snapping her out of her reverie.

"Oh, yes. Sorry, Princess!" she shuffled after me, nearly slipping on the smooth steps as we climbed the staircase to my bedchamber.

As per what I'd seen already, even the halls on the second floor were wider and more extravagant than at our castle in Capthar.

They must be a lot more financially sound than we are, I thought.

Just from what I had seen so far, that seemed to be the case. There must have been big reasons why King Leopold did what he did: kidnapping girls, training a new princess... killing Joseph and imprisoning Janice... That had to be a part of it, and it made me sick.

"This is your room, Princess," the maid said to me. Her voice matched her weak-looking body. She turned the doorknob to the enormous door before us. It had magnificent carvings of flowers and vines in the wood. The Polartians really knew what it meant to pay attention to detail.

"Thank you, Clara." I gave her a big smile. She flushed, probably not used to being thanked so kindly. She curtsied and hurried away.

My room was at *least* twice as big as my chamber in Mardasia.

"Oh, my heavens," Minerva gasped. She ran her finger along the purple wallpaper then hurried to the bed and stroked the quilts resting upon my *giant* mattress.

After a little more exploration, we found a guest bedroom attached to my powder room.

"This must be where I'm staying," Minerva said, giddily examining her own fireplace and various sofas. It was significantly smaller than the main chamber, but it had to be the same size as mine in Capthar.

"Is this not exciting, Amelia?" Minerva said to me, noticing the scowl on my face.

I couldn't tell her that I felt angry, depressed, sick... I couldn't tell her that despite all those swirling emotions, I felt completely numb and impervious to everything around me. I just really didn't care, but then I did. *Janice...*

"Of course, Lady Minerva," I said.

In that moment, a rap on the door sounded.

"That must be our luggage! Let's get you out of your travel clothes and ready for dinner," Minerva said to me.

"How is your pork, Princess Amelia?"

I looked up from my plate to the Queen who sat at the head of the table. I was on her left, and the Prince sat across from me on her right. The only others at dinner were Lady Minerva and those serving us.

"It's wonderful, Your Majesty," I replied.

The Prince glanced at me over his fork. We made eye contact. His eyes were a bright green, like his mother's. I knew he was three years my senior, he being twenty-two, but the glasses made him look my age. He gave me a quick smile and went back to his food. He seemed so curious about me, yet shy.

Minerva nudged me under the table with her foot. I shot a look at her, annoyed. She gestured her head a bit towards the Prince, encouraging me to talk with him. I groaned, but caught myself, clearing my throat to cover the sound.

"Prince Alexander," I said after dabbing my mouth with the ivory napkin on my lap, "I'm excited to get to know you a little better."

The Prince chuckled a bit. "As am I, Princess Amelia." He didn't look away from his plate, poking at his potatoes with his fork.

That was irritating.

Minerva kicked me again. She had told me earlier that it was important I woo the man, even though we were already betrothed. The thought of any type of flirtation made me want to curl up in a ball and cry.

"Your palace is beautiful," I said to both the Queen and Prince. "I assume the gardens are just as breathtaking. I would love to see them sometime."

The Prince perked up at that a bit. "I can show you around. Walking among the grounds is one of my favorite things to do." The eye contact he gave me lasted more than our normal two seconds.

I forced a smile on my lips. "That would be marvelous."

The Queen was studying me intensely. I shivered under her gaze.

"Tomorrow morning then," Prince Alexander said, getting excited.

I tilted my head, trying to look cute, and nodded. Out of the corner of my eye, I could see Minerva giving me an approving smile.

Chapter 20

A manservant led me to the back entrance of the castle. The sun was rising, and the light glinted warmly through the various windows along our path.

"His Highness told me to take you all the way out to the gardens, Princess," the man said. He was a very tall, scrawny man, and his powdered wig made it all the funnier.

"Is he already there?"

"I believe so, Princess. He goes out there most mornings."

I didn't know much about Prince Alexander yet, but what I had learned so far wasn't very appealing to me. He seemed so reserved and was a bit, dare I say, odd.

The hallway we were headed down quickly turned from stone walls to a line of trellises decorated with vines and other shrubbery, making a tunnel. The light from outside became stronger the further we followed the path, giving me a better view of the outside. A maze of short, well-groomed hedges spun around the spacious area, and there was a large gazebo in the center, strung with bright flowers. It was breathtaking, and the land went further than I could even see. The man-servant and I both looked around, unable to find the Prince, until he shouted out to us. Swiveling my head to the right, I saw his distant figure waving to me under a smaller gazebo that sat directly in the middle of a large pond.

My escort bowed deeply, his nose almost hitting the floor. It was quite... extravagant.

"If I may, Princess?"

I nodded, dismissing him, and began the trek to the Prince. Reaching the edge of the pond, I surveyed the situation, confused.

"Your Highness, how do I get over there?" I shouted over the water.

Prince Alexander looked up from the book he was studying, sunlight reflecting off his spectacles, nearly blinding me.

"Oh, there's a boat here," he said, then went back to his book.

I bit my lip. "The boat next to you way over there?" I tried to hide the frustration in my voice.

The Prince looked over his shoulder to see the boat tied to the gazebo's small deck.

"Oh, yeah," he said. "I'll come to you, Princess."

"Thanks," I muttered under my breath.

I watched as the Prince clumsily got into the small rowboat. After a second or two, he steadied himself and tucked his book under the seat. He rowed over to me, which took longer than what I really had patience for, but I kept a smile on my face.

"Sorry about that," he said, flushed from the exertion.

"That is alright, Your Highness."

"Please," he said, "call me Alexander."

That was a relief. "You can call me Mi— Amelia." My heart pounded from the near mistake, but he didn't seem to notice.

"I think that will help us feel a bit more comfortable with each other, not being so formal." He smiled a crooked smile. He definitely seemed more confident than the night before.

"I agree," I said.

"Great!" Alexander clapped his hands together enthusiastically. "I wanted to show you around our gardens. As you can probably tell, there's a *lot* to see, so let's get started."

He reached under the seat of the rowboat for his book, then offered his other arm to me. I took it, and we walked.

"You know, I'm not much of a people person."

"Oh?" I said, keeping my eyes forward.

"I often find solitude out here, by myself. I don't like socializing much."

I thought about how shy he acted towards me last night, around a bunch of other people. Out here, it was just us.

"You seem to be doing okay right now."

He chuckled. "I'm *supposed* to try to with you. On the inside, I'm terrified."

I didn't say anything. Maybe it was because I

was scared, too. I was scared for other, more extreme reasons.

We walked in silence, and I tried to look as if I was interested in other things than a conversation. I stared at a bright yellow butterfly that flew around my head, looked intently at the various plants and flowers, anything to distract me from what was happening.

"You see that tree down there," Alexander said, pointing far ahead of the stone path.

I followed his finger to see a small, knotted tree that looked nearly dead. It was very different from its surroundings.

"It's my favorite tree. It doesn't look like much, but my father and I planted it when I was about four. He said it would be our special tree, and we climbed it together for years before he... before he died."

I caught some sadness in the Prince's eyes and felt empathetic. Minerva told me not to mention the King or his demise, but Alexander had brought it up.

"I know what it's like to lose a father," I said.

"Huh?" he said.

My eyes widened as I tried to come up with a recovery. "Uh, I mean, I can *imagine* what it's like to lose a father. My mother died when I was very young," I said, remembering to be Amelia, not myself. Although, Milly had lost *both* parents to various fates.

Alexander nodded. "I heard about that," he said.

"Looks like we have *some* things in common, at least." He smiled at me again. It was a cute smile, and I found myself smiling back.

"I thought we could try climbing the tree today," he said.

"What?"

He laughed. "Come on, it'll be super fun! It's so easy. That tree was *built* for climbing."

"My dress!" I exclaimed.

"Oh, yeah," he said, pulling his arm away from mine to study my outfit. "Hm... Try tying it up out of your way."

I gaped at him. "People are going to see!"

He shook his head. "The tree is far enough down the path. No one can see it from the castle."

I just stood there, cocking an eyebrow at the Prince.

"It'll be an adventure!" he said. "Come on!"

I watched as he ran down the path towards his little tree, shaking my head.

Whatever, I thought, and then proceeded to run after him, hiking my skirts up above my ankles.

It was quite the run, being that the tree was pretty far out there. We stood next to each other for a minute after reaching the tree, both out of breath.

"The gardeners always ask if they can cut this tree down, but I never let them."

I looked up at its branches. There were no leaves and the wood looked almost rotted. It was also a lot bigger than what I had first perceived. I could see why the gardeners wanted to get rid of it.

"Here, I'll give you a boost," he said, setting his book on the grass and squatting with his hands out as a foothold. He was serious.

I sighed, giving in, and kicked my shoes off and tied up my dress through my legs. I was lucky to have been dressed in a lighter weight, outdoor dress this morning. He boosted me up with his hands until I found some good handholds on the bark. I scaled the tree quickly, having done things like this a lot as a child.

"You're good at this!" Alexander shouted up to me. "I didn't think a princess would be!"

"Maybe not a princess, but Milly is," I whispered, actually beginning to enjoy myself.

Alexander began to climb up the tree after I found a sturdy-looking branch to sit on. He quickly found a branch near mine and sat as well.

"I used to pretend this tree was a portal to another world," he said, lounging back onto his branch comfortably. "A world like the ones I read in books, where there are elves and fairies and magic."

I laid back on my branch, too, allowing the bark and the cool breeze to tangle the locks Minerva had laboriously put into my hair. Alexander craned his neck a bit and started watching me.

"You're different from other women."

I sat up, confused. "What does that mean, exactly?"

He shook his head. "I mean no offense. It's just

that most of the other noblewomen are so forceful and... pompous." He moved his gaze back to the clear, blue sky.

I found myself laughing, despite myself. He laughed, too.

"I know what you mean," I said.

"I like that you're different, though." He ran his fingers through his golden hair. "It makes it easier to talk to you."

"I'm glad," I said, smiling at him.

"There's something else." He sat up to study me further. "When you smile, it's so warm and... lovely, but there's something in your eyes that I've never seen before—like a certain mystery and darkness. It's fascinating."

I clenched my jaw, reminded of why I was there. Was my pain really so obvious?

"I'm sorry," he said, noticing the frown on my face. "I didn't mean to insult you in any way."

I shook my head. "No, it's fine. I'm just feeling a little lightheaded. Maybe it's best we head back for now."

He squinted his eyes at me, confused, but nodded. He climbed down the tree and waited at the bottom to provide me any needed help. I accepted his outstretched hand and gingerly set foot on the grass. He rushed over to grab my shoes as I untied my dress and brushed it down with my hands.

"Thank you," I said as he helped me slide the shoes on my feet.

"Of course," he replied.

I slid my arm in the crook of his, and we began to head back to the castle. We walked in silence, and I tried desperately to push away my thoughts of Joseph and my sister. It was vital that I stay put together.

After reaching the back entrance, Alexander broke the silence.

"May I escort you back to your room, Amelia?" he asked. "You look rather pale."

I almost refused, but I knew I'd get an earful from Minerva for doing that.

"Yes, thank you," I said.

We shared a couple of pleasantries here and there as he walked me back to my chamber, and he pointed out various portraits of his ancestors and told me bits and pieces of their stories. I had a hard time paying attention.

"I had a lot of fun today," Alexander said when we got to my door. "Thank you for spending it with me." He studied my face, brow furrowed. "Should I call a doctor?"

I shook my head. "Oh, no. I will just lie down for a spell. I'll see you at dinner."

He grinned. "I hope you'll be feeling better soon. Maybe I'll make you climb a banister next time."

I laughed, a real laugh. Every once in a while, this guy could get to me. It felt good to laugh.

"Thank you for today," I said, curtsying. He opened my door for me and bowed in return.

"Well?" Minerva said as soon as the door closed

behind me. I jumped.

"You frightened me!" I said. She was sitting on the edge of my bed, as if she had been waiting for me the entire time.

"How did it go? I hope it went well because you were only gone for an hour!"

I sighed. "It went very well. But I did walk a lot, so I would like to rest for a little while."

Minerva seemed dissatisfied with that answer, but, surprisingly, she nodded in agreement.

"It'll be good to rest up for more courting tonight," she said, and then stepped out of the main room to her own to give me some privacy.

I sighed in relief and pulled my dress over my head. I plopped onto my mattress in just a shift and stared up at the ceiling. So many different emotions were spinning inside me in that moment. I wanted to scream, I wanted to laugh, I wanted to cry! Everything in me didn't want to enjoy my outing with Alexander, but I did. Despite everything, he was sweet and funny. But how could I even *begin* to become friends with someone who didn't know everything about me was a lie? I blinked out a tear and let myself drift off to sleep.

Chapter 21

"Wake up, Princess Amelia!"

I jolted at the feeling of Minerva's long finger-nails digging into my bare arms as she shook me awake.

"What time is it?" I asked, yawning.

"Time for you to find the Prince and flirt with him some more!" She ripped the warm covers from my body, and I shivered in the cold air.

I glanced out the window. It couldn't have been much later than dawn.

"But I'll see him later for tea. And heaven knows you taught me how to do *that* well."

Minerva struck me on the top of my head with her palm.

"Ouch!" I cried, rubbing at it.

Minerva got me dressed in what seemed to be under thirty seconds and shooed me out the door before I could say, "What about breakfast?"

I took my time exploring the castle, feeling no rush to find the Prince like Minerva had urged me to. I stopped at a large statue after wandering for about ten minutes and studied it. It was chis-eled out of gray stone and sanded down to an unimaginable smoothness. The image was stunning — a large man stood regally with his longsword held in the air triumphantly. His long robes were carved to look as if they were blowing gently in the wind, and his crown glinted as if real. It was so life-like. I read the inscription at the bottom and read, "In Honor of Our King Philip."

Alexander's father, I thought. I stared at the stone face and could recognize the similarities between father and son. They had the same, strong nose and pointed chin. And, even in stone, I could tell they had the same kindness in their eyes, which was something Alexander's mother definitely lacked.

The sound of grunts and swords clanging to my right interrupted my thoughts. Curious, I headed in the direction of the noise to find a large, open doorway and two men in an intense duel with one another. Upon closer inspection, I noticed one to be Prince Alexander. They didn't seem to notice me as I watched. It was incredible. Alexander seemed more light on his feet and more at ease than what I had previously perceived him to be. The clumsiness was gone, and it was like the athleticism of a sword fight was where he was himself. As I watched him deflect blow after blow and strike his opponent, I was amazed at the dexterity and strength in his body. His muscles flexed as he approached his opponent again, and his sweat glistened on his forehead. It was like I was watching a completely different person, and it was very attractive.

I shook my head, face growing hot, and chastised myself for thinking about my sudden attraction to him.

"Princess."

I gasped, not having noticed that the dueling had stopped and both men were staring at me.

Alexander smiled and gestured for me to enter the room.

"I will be going, Your Highness." The other man said. He must have been a soldier, considering his build and the way he had just fought.

"Of course, Sir Paul. Thank you for the bout. Same time tomorrow?"

Sir Paul nodded, bowing to each of us in turn, and turned on his heel to leave us alone.

I looked around the room, gasping at the brilliant chandeliers hanging above us.

"This room is enormous!" I exclaimed, smiling as my voice echoed against the walls. "Is this where the soldiers train?"

Alexander laughed. "No. This is just one of the ballrooms. Soldiers do most of their training outside."

"Oh," I said, feeling slightly embarrassed. "You're very good. At sword fighting, I mean"

Alexander flushed a little, some of his normal quirkiness coming out again.

"Thanks," he said. "It's another thing my father and I did together before he passed away."

"Climbing trees and sword fighting," I listed on

my fingers.

"Not to mention wrestling."

My jaw fell open. "A king, wrestling?"

He laughed. "My father was a very good king, but he also knew how important it is to have fun. Does your father feel the same way?"

I thought about my own father, but then remembered he was asking about King Leopold. I shuffled my feet, feeling uncomfortable.

"I think so," I said, lying. "He does work really hard, though. I don't see him often."

Alexander nodded, growing solemn. "My mother works hard. She is very different from who my father was, but she is good for the kingdom."

I cocked my head at him. He was being very open with me. I inched closer to him, trying to decide if I should comfort him. Before I could put an arm on his shoulder, the doors on the other side of the room burst open, and Queen Andromeda strode in, red dress trailing behind her in a never-ending train. Her long, raven hair was done up into a tower on the top of her head. She never failed to look as extravagant as possible.

Alexander next to me visibly cowered a little smaller, and he pushed his spectacles back up his nose. Within those few seconds, all of his clumsy awkwardness had come back.

Interesting, I thought.

"Oh, splendid," the Queen said, clapping her hands together. "You two should join me for breakfast. I hate eating alone."

Chapter 22

The next few weeks consisted of so many things *all* with Prince Alexander. Horseback riding, playing chess, reading books together (he especially loved that one)... And I was actually starting to warm up to him more and more. He was kind of endearing in his own, unique way. At the very least, I thought he and I could become great friends, and I was grateful for that.

We were sitting in the library in silence. I was reading a very boring book about the Kingdom of Polart's taxing system, which actually seemed rather sound, and he was reading another one of his fantasy books.

"Is that good?" I asked him.

He nodded, not moving his eyes away from the pages. "It's about a woman who falls in love with an elf," he said.

I snorted. "Aren't elves supposed to be short?"

He kept on reading as I laughed at him. "Not in this story. They're actually relatively taller than humans in this book."

He turned the page, and I looked over his shoulder. I started reading a paragraph about this woman and the elf-man receiving each other in a passionate kiss.

"Wow, there's a lot of romance in there. I thought men were more of the type to read books about war and blood," I teased.

He actually looked up at me, away from his book, eyes dancing humorously. "Most men don't even read like I do, Amelia. That being the case, I can read whatever I feel like reading."

He winked at me, and I chuckled at how clumsy it was. He blushed.

"I'm hungry," Alexander said, changing the subject. He set his book down and stretched.

"Should we ask someone to fetch some food?" I asked, setting my book down, as well.

He shook his head. "I like getting things myself whenever I can. I'll be back." Alexander scooted his chair back and stood up. "Do you want anything?"

"No," I said.

"Suit yourself. I'll be back."

I sat by myself in the quiet room, admiring my surroundings. There were cases upon cases of books and documents that piled all the way to the tall ceiling of the library.

I heard some footsteps near the entrance. "Back already?" I said, swirling my head around, but it wasn't Alexander.

"Princess Amelia," the Queen said. She walked towards me, her long, emerald dress flowing delicately against the carpeted floor.

I stood up hurriedly and curtsied. "Your Majesty. I thought you were—"

Queen Andromeda raised her hand to quiet me. "I know, dear. You and my son have been spending a lot of time together. Please, sit." She gestured for me to take my chair again.

"Thank you," I said. A visit from the Queen was nothing to make light of. I shoved my hands in my lap to keep them from shaking.

The Queen came closer and took Alexander's empty seat. She studied me for what seemed to be an eternity. Her deep, green eyes held such an intensity in her gaze. I shifted uncomfortably in my seat.

"Tell me, Princess. How are you feeling about your betrothal?"

I gulped. Was she interrogating me? "I am grateful for the blessing it is for our kingdom," I said.

"Well said." The Queen ran her finger along the edges of the book Alexander had been reading, looking thoughtful. "I heard you took very ill recently. You were so indisposed that many of your subjects believed you to have run away," she said to me, almost whispering.

I felt my palms sweating. Did she know? What brought on this conversation?

"I *was* very ill and hadn't made an appearance in court for almost two weeks. And people spread all kinds of silly rumors about the royal family all the time. I'm sure it is the same way here."

Queen Andromeda raised a dark brow at me. I

bowed my head, embarrassed.

"I am glad to see you are well then."

I nodded. "Thank you, Your Majesty."

She stood up, and I followed suit.

"Please, stay seated. You may go back to your reading." She gestured towards my book in front of me.

Before I could thank her, she swept out of the room swiftly, yet elegantly. I breathed out a sigh of relief, happy for that to be over.

Queen Andromeda briskly left the library, thoughts churning violently. She had heard things, disturbing things, that had prompted her to talk with Princess Amelia. She hadn't known what to ask, exactly, but the conversation brought upon even more suspicion. The Princess answered all of her questions quickly, but had been unable to hide how nervous she was.

The Queen turned the corner quickly and looked around to make sure she wasn't being followed. She stepped over to the wall on her left and waited patiently. Not thirty seconds later, an older man came into view and saw the Queen. He signaled to her, showing he hadn't been followed, and approached her quietly.

"Your Majesty," he said, bowing.

"Clarence. Anymore news?" The Queen urged.

The man grinned, causing his wrinkles to further distort his aged face. "Upon further investigation, I found more evidence."

She shook her head. "The Princess just told me that she was ill, and that her people were spreading silly rumors."

Clarence chuckled. "I don't think it's just a rumor. After the Princess Amelia supposedly ran away, there were a few disappearances of some young women not even a day later."

"So?" Queen Andromeda said.

"So... I have some connections that say those missing young women were contestants, if you will, to become the Princess Amelia as if she had never left."

The Queen tapped her fingers on the wall next to her. "Are your connections reliable?"

Clarence winked at her. "You know they are. Some of my connections fixed your little problem with your husband, didn't they?"

The Queen raised a finger to her lips. "Not so loud," she hissed.

The old man giggled, and Queen Andromeda rolled her eyes.

"How am I even supposed to prove she is an impostor?" she said.

Clarence came even closer, and she could smell the alcohol on his breath. "I know someone."

Chapter 23

I woke up in the morning to find that a note had been slid under my door. I picked up the parchment and unfolded it in my hands.

"Meet me at the pond," it read. His handwriting was big and elegant. "Don't worry, I'll actually row you over to the gazebo this time."

I smiled. Prince Alexander was giving me notes now? He never ceased to surprise me.

"What's that?"

I jumped and whirled around. Minerva was always sneaking up on me.

"I'm supposed to rendezvous with the Prince," I said after catching my breath from the fright.

She nodded. "Good. You've been courting each other for over a month now. Best to hurry things along, Princess Amelia. He needs to propose to you."

"Propose?" I said, putting the note down on my bedside table. "I thought we were already engaged."

Minerva walked over to the wardrobe to pick out a gown for me. "Technically, you are just betrothed. It still needs to be made official, and then there will be an engagement ball, I'm sure, and—"

"Oh, my goodness," I said, falling onto my bed, feeling exhausted again.

"Up!" Lady Minerva shouted to me, holding up an atrocious, bright yellow dress. "We cannot keep His Highness waiting!"

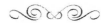

Alexander was waiting for me at the edge of the big pond in the castle gardens. I waved to him and sped up my pace.

"Good morning, Amelia," he said. He grabbed my hand and kissed it awkwardly.

I laughed. "What was that?"

He shrugged, blushing. "I was just trying it out." He gestured for me to take a seat in the little row-boat. "I thought I'd actually take you to that gazebo today."

I lifted my skirts and stepped carefully into the boat, Alexander following suit. It wobbled a bit, but we both made it in safe. Alexander picked up the oars and began to row us over to the gazebo.

"This is gorgeous," I whispered in awe, staring at the water. There were dozens of colorful fish swimming below me, and their scales sparkled prettily in the sunlight.

"It really is," he replied. Something told me he wasn't really talking about the view. I shifted my feet, suddenly feeling uncomfortable.

Alexander got out of the boat first, then helped me out onto the small deck. I walked into the gazebo as he tied the boat to a post.

"It's so quiet here," I said. "I can see why you like it so much."

He nodded. "It's a sanctuary for me. Sometimes I feel like I really need to escape."

"Why would you ever want to escape life?" I teased.

Alexander smiled, but he seemed nervous.

I cocked my head to the side. "You okay?"

He nodded, straightening his glasses.

"Did you know that we're not actually officially engaged?" I said, remembering my conversation with Minerva. I laughed, trying to lighten the mood. "Apparently, you have to actually propose."

Alexander's jaw dropped, and he stared at me, dumbfounded.

"Uh...What did I say?" I prodded.

He stood like a statue for a long time, but then he burst out laughing.

"You ruined it!" he exclaimed.

"Ruined what?" I stepped back from him, confused.

"I was just about to propose to you!" He reached into his back pocket and pulled out a magnificent golden ring encrusted in the shiniest diamonds I had ever seen.

"What?" I squeaked.

He brushed it off. "It's way better this way. Now *this* is a proposal I would've expected to happen to me!"

I couldn't hear his words. I just stared at the ring in his hand, blood rushing in my ears. It was real. It must have not hit me until now: I was supposed to get married. I was supposed to get married to a Prince who didn't know my real name. I was a fake! I was only here to protect my sister! I was only here because... Joseph... my vision started to go black, and I stumbled. Alexander rushed over to steady me.

"Amelia?" he said, but his voice sounded so distant.

"Yes," I found myself saying. I wouldn't let them kill my sister. I would go along with this forever, just for her sake.

"Yes to marrying me?" he asked.

My mouth was dry, so I just nodded.

"Amelia, are you okay?"

I shook myself out of my thoughts and forced a smile. "Yes, sorry. It just felt real to me all of a sudden."

"I know the feeling," he said, smiling back.

No, you really don't, I thought.

Chapter 24

It was the dead of night as the Queen slipped out of the side entrance from the kitchens. She hugged her black cloak tight around her face and tiptoed away from the castle. There weren't many guards on this side, because it was the servant's quarters, but she was careful not to make any noise all the same.

Following the directions Clarence had given her, Andromeda found the street leading to her destination.

"She lives on the west side of the town square," the old man had told her.

After a long walk, the Queen started to see the buildings that surrounded the center of their capital. She had been to town square before, when travelling or giving public appearances, but never alone and *never* by foot.

After another few minutes of walking, Andromeda saw the tent that Clarence had described to her, if you could call it that. It was really just a few ratted, old rugs tied and hanging across a few large sticks staked into the ground.

The Queen took a deep breath and approached

the structure. She saw a light flickering inside, and a small, huddled figure. Andromeda cleared her throat.

"Excuse me," she said, only loud enough for the person inside to hear.

The person whipped their head to the sound, and Andromeda gasped at the grotesqueness of the woman before her: she was covered in scars and dirt, and the little gray hair left on her head was about to fall out.

"Is that our dear Queen Andromeda?" the woman whistled through broken teeth.

Andromeda, eyes wide, nodded.

"Enter, enter!" The woman excitedly moved some things around and pulled up a chair for the Queen.

The Queen took the chair cautiously, but only after using her cloak to wipe it as clean as possible.

"I knew you would come," the woman said. She took her seat across from the Queen and continued eating her bowl of peas at the little barrel she used as a table.

Andromeda raised an eyebrow, but chose to ignore that statement. "I was told you could help me with a certain problem I have."

"Depends on the problem," the old lady said through mouthfuls of food.

The Queen scowled at the pieces of food that landed on the barrel in front of her as the woman spoke. "I need to prove that someone is really who they say they are."

The woman nodded. "You want to prove the Princess Amelia really *is* Princess Amelia."

The Queen was taken aback. "How—"

"Exactly how I know that you were the one that plotted your husband's death."

"How dare you—"

"Or how you want to rule the kingdom, but your son getting married will ruin those plans. But," the witch raised a crooked, knobby finger, "you don't want to kill your son like you did the King. That's why when you heard a rumor that the sweet Princess might be a fake, you want to jump at the opportunity to try and sever their betrothal."

The Queen's jaw dropped.

"I'm a witch, dear," the woman said, turning her attention back to her food. "I know things."

It took a moment for Andromeda to find words. "You can help me then? I can pay you very handsomely."

The witch guffawed, spitting more peas out towards the Queen. "I never questioned whether or not you could pay me!"

"Fine," Andromeda said, annoyed. "Name your price."

"A time will come when you will pay your price." The woman stared thoughtfully at the Queen. Andromeda shivered.

"Please," the Queen said. "I'll pay whatever you want. Just help me."

The witch looked around the space and then

back to her peas, then she started giggling uncontrollably. She dipped a wrinkled hand into the bowl and fished out one of the peas with her long, yellowed fingernails. The woman closed her eyes and chanted something incomprehensible to the Queen's ears.

"Here you go," the witch said, grinning from ear to ear. She dropped the pea onto the makeshift table in front of the Queen.

Andromeda stared at it. "What in heaven's name will that do?"

"You place it under her mattress."

"That really clears it up, thank you."

The witch nodded, ignoring the Queen's sarcasm. "Yup. If she is the real Princess, she won't be able to sleep a wink. But if she's an impostor, as soon as she hits the pillow, she will be out for exactly 12 hours, as if in a coma."

The Queen stroked her chin, studying the pea before her. "Interesting."

"There are some rules, though," the witch said, waving her spoon at the Queen. "You have to put it under her mattress immediately after she lies down, or it won't work. *And* it only has one use."

"Well... that may be difficult."

The witch shrugged. "I only provide the magic, I don't do the plotting."

Andromeda pulled out a very large coin purse from inside her cloak and poured out a large pile of coins.

"Will that do for payment?" the Queen asked.

The witch didn't even seem phased by the pile of money. "Like I said, your time will come when you pay your price."

"Just keep it," the Queen said, tucking the pea gently into a pocket inside the cloak. "And if this doesn't work, remember that I am your Queen, and I can bring you hell."

The witch smiled and winked. "It'll work."

Chapter 25

I lay in my bed, exhausted from a full day's worth of horseback riding with not just Prince Alexander, but what felt like the entire court. My mouth hurt from smiling and saying one "thank you" after another from what seemed to be a thousand "Congratulations on your engagement!" For those who think princesses have it easy, they really don't.

"You need to get out of that bed, Princess!" Lady Minerva snapped at me as she walked into the room. "Really, you must spend half the time lying down!"

I groaned. "I just sat on a horse and socialized for three hours, Lady Minerva."

"Princesses don't talk back!" Minerva grabbed my hands and pulled me into a sitting position. "The engagement ball is in less than two hours, and we have a lot to do to make you presentable." She scowled at my dirty clothes and tangled hair from the ride. "I already drew you a bath. Disrobe."

I rolled my eyes as soon as her back was turned, but slipped out of my riding clothes like a good princess should. I followed Minerva to the powder room and slid into the warm water.

"Don't get your hair wet!" she snapped at me as I was about to slide my whole body under the water. "There's no way we'll dry it on time! I'll make do with it as it is."

It was hard to relax in a bath when a snobby woman was yanking at the tangles in your hair with a comb.

"Out," she ordered me.

I stepped out of the bath and allowed her to wrap a warm robe around me. Minerva then trotted out of the room, leaving me alone for a moment in front of the looking glass. I looked at my eyes, finding the darkness Alexander had mentioned on that day. It hadn't always been there.

"Here." Minerva came in holding an elegant, light blue gown decorated with a pretty lace and some pearl beading.

"It's beautiful," I said, happy to see a dress not nearly as cumbersome and poofy as others she had forced onto my body in the past.

She looked at it, seemingly pleased with herself. "I picked this one out, thinking it would match your blue eyes and blonde hair very well."

I was surprised by the compliment. "Thank you, Lady Minerva."

She helped me slide into a shift then pulled the dress over my head. I was pleased with what I saw in the mirror. The dress flattered my figure, and, like Minerva said, was a good match to my eyes and hair.

"Eh, I guess it'll do." And just like that, the bonding moment was over. "Let's do something with that mop on your head, and then we'll work on your face."

Lady Minerva led me to the vanity in the main bedroom and with a preheated fireplace poker, she carefully curled my hair around it. It was crazy what royalty did to look pretty. I still wasn't and never *could* get used to it. Then came the rouge, powder, and the perfume. I coughed at the smell of all three.

"You're done!" Minerva said. "And just in time, too!"

"Are you not going to get ready?" I asked her.

She looked down at her lime green dress and smoothed her slick, black hair that always ended in a tight bun on the top of her head.

"I *am* ready," she said, glaring at me.

"Oh."

Minerva sighed. "Let's just go."

The ball was a million times more extravagant than the one King Leopold threw before I left. There were at least twice the amount of people, and the decor was stunning. Banners with the red and purple Polart colors were strung about the

ballroom and there were beautiful, silver cande-
labras adorning every side of the room. Dinner
wasn't being served like at King Leopold's parties,
but there were numerous tables scattered all over
the place carrying mountains of food for people
to pick at as they pleased. My stomach rumbled.
I was about to make my way over to one of the
tables when Minerva pulled at my arm.

"You haven't been introduced yet," she hissed in
my ear.

We stood at the front of the ballroom, and apparently I had to stay there until Prince Alexander arrived, and then we could be introduced as a
newly engaged couple. And that, of course, was ridiculous to me. Everybody already knew we were
engaged. Actually, I was pretty sure most of those
people went riding with us that morning and gave
their congratulations then.

"Thanks for waiting," Alexander whispered in
my ear.

I craned my neck to look back at him. "Did I
have a choice?"

He laughed, offering his arm to me. "No."

Queen Andromeda had come in with Alexander. She didn't even look at me.

"Lords and ladies!" a burly man wearing purple
tights shouted to the crowd, silencing them.
"Queen Andromeda."

The crowd applauded as she stepped deeper
into the room. It was our turn next.

"And announcing, for the first time, Prince

Alexander, and his fiancée Princess Amelia of Mardasia.

Cheers erupted all around me. The sound was overwhelming. After the cheers died down, the musicians in the corner began to play a soft tune, and Alexander turned me to look at him.

"May I have this dance?" he asked.

I nodded and allowed him to lead me to the dance floor. He put his hand on my waist, and I rested mine on his shoulder. He tried to lead me to the music, but was failing miserably. His eyes darted around the room. He seemed embarrassed, knowing people were watching us.

"Here," I whispered, "Just follow my lead. One, two, three. One, two, three... There you go!"

"I'm glad one of us can dance," he said. "I never had the knack for it."

I laughed, but then was hit with a flashback of Joseph sweeping me across the dance floor with ease and strength. I shifted my eyes to the floor, trying to hide the sudden sadness I felt, but Alexander caught it. He was silent for a moment, but then spoke:

"Is the idea of marrying me really that bad?"

"What?" I said, looking up at him.

"You always seem to be warming up to me and having fun, but then you have these moments where you seem to lose all of that and... you seem so sad."

"No!" I tried to assure him. "It's not you, I'm just... I can't explain."

Alexander let go of my waist. "How about I go get us some drinks," he said, bowing.

"Alexander—"

But he had already walked away from me. I sighed. It wasn't his fault at all. I had to let him know that somehow.

"Lords and ladies!" the announcer at the front bellowed again. "Announcing King Leopold of Mardasia!"

My heart sank as I whirled around to see, and there he was, regal as always. A maroon robe spilled over his shoulders and brushed the dark boots on his feet. His large, golden crown (something that would only ever fit on *his* large head), glinted in the light. He looked around to find my face. We made eye contact, and he gave me a beaming smile. I felt like I was going to throw up. People parted out of his way as he moved towards me.

"Daughter!" he cried, pulling me into a hug. "Congratulations!"

I had never seen him so... jovial, but as I looked into his eyes, there was still a lack of emotion. It was rare that he ever let his eyes give him away, but there were a few times when he did. Like when he killed Joseph.

"Thank you, Father," I finally choked out.

"And this must be the lucky Prince!"

I hadn't noticed Alexander walk up to us, two drinks in hand.

He bowed. "Your Majesty."

King Leopold beamed. "This is an historic day!"

I smiled back, trying to keep from shaking nervously. Alexander handed me one of the drinks, and I gulped it down eagerly. I didn't normally drink alcohol, given that my *real* father was a drunk, but the wretchedness about this situation made it seem rather appealing. I yearned for *something* to get me through the lies and pain.

"Uh…" Alexander said. "Would you like me to get you another one?"

"Oh, no." I forced a smile. "I can get one myself. I would like to eat some food, anyway."

I made my way over to one of the tables with food, happy to get away for a moment. I really had been hungry earlier, but the arrival of my "father" had made me lose my appetite. I gestured for a servant to pour me another drink.

I watched from the corner as Alexander spoke with King Leopold and various other passersby on the floor. The shy version of the Prince was coming out again, and I could see him shuffling his feet with anxiety. Leopold looked up from their conversation and gave me a quick look. I knew what that look meant: "Behave yourself."

I gulped down a third drink, not very princesslike, I'm sure, and headed back to my fiancé's side. I was grateful for the tingling sensation of the alcohol. Leopold had already headed away to socialize with Queen Andromeda, who stood by herself watching the partygoers with her nose turned up in the air.

"You came back fast," Alexander said to me.

I slid my arm through his. "Alexander, I'm sorry. It's just been a little bit overwhelming. You know, with so many people around. And I've never been engaged before."

He laughed. "Me neither." He winked at me, and it was oddly comforting. "Maybe we should get away from all the people for a bit. I know *I* would like that."

He led me to the edge of the room to a large balcony. We stepped out into the cool air outside. The sound of the party was still loud behind us, but more bearable. I breathed deeply through my nose.

"This is a lot better," I said.

I heard Alexander sigh in relief next to me. "Agreed."

I stepped over to the edge and leaned over the railing, overlooking the grounds.

"You look beautiful tonight." Alexander stepped beside me and lightly touched his shoulder against mine.

I was not expecting him to say that. "Thank you," I whispered.

He raised his fingers to stroke my cheek, and it felt as if my heart would pound out of my chest. I couldn't decide what I was feeling.

"You know, I was very skeptical about this arrangement in the beginning." He turned my face to look into my eyes. "But..." He hesitated, and I held my breath. "I think I've fallen in love with you."

I froze and almost didn't notice him moving to

kiss me. The warmth from his lips was intoxicating, and I felt myself wrap my arms around him, but then my eyes flew open. I felt sick to my stomach. It wasn't right. Just a month ago I had watched King Leopold kill Joseph right in front of me, and on top of that, Alexander wasn't in love with *me*, he was in love with *Amelia*.

Alexander pulled back and pressed his forehead against mine. He had a goofy grin on his face, and it made me feel even more guilty.

"I love you," he said.

I took a deep breath, trying to decide what to say. The tingling sensation from the alcohol wasn't helping me get my thoughts together. I thought of Janice again... After what seemed like years, I finally knew what I had to do.

"I love you, too." I forced a smile, and swallowed down the lump in my throat.

Chapter 26

Minerva and I were headed back to our bed-chambers. The party hadn't quite ended, but we wanted to beat the rush of people leaving to go back to their homes and rooms. King Leopold had approached before we left, saying he was headed back to Mardasia immediately. He had then given me another warning look, but I was in a daze. I couldn't stop thinking about what Alexander had said—what I had said! I did not know if I loved him or not, but I did know hurting him was one of the last things I wanted to do.

Suddenly hearing footsteps behind us, we turned.

"Princess Amelia, Lady Minerva." Queen Andromeda said as she approached us. Why did she always turn up at the strangest times?

We curtsied to the Queen. "Your Majesty," Minerva and I said simultaneously.

"If I may, Lady Minerva, I would like to walk the Princess to her chambers alone." The Queen waved her hand to Minerva in dismissal.

"Yes, of course." Minerva curtsied again and scurried back in the direction of the party.

I reluctantly watched Lady Minerva walk away, afraid to be with the cold Queen by myself again.

We walked in complete silence to my room, and I couldn't help but wring my hands nervously.

"Allow me." The Queen reached for the doorknob to my chamber and pulled the door open.

"Thank you, Your Majesty." I stepped into the dark room.

"Here, I'll light a candle." I watched, curious, as Queen Andromeda searched the room for a tinderbox. "Do you have anything to drink?" she asked after she lit a candle on the mantle of the fireplace.

"Um, yes, there's some brandy on my bedside table."

She walked in that direction. "Would you care for a drink, too?"

I thought about the three drinks I had already had, but was afraid to refuse. She poured some of the brandy into the two small glasses next to the bottle and walked over to me.

"Let's sit." She gestured to one of the sofas in the room. I took my drink from her hand and followed her to sit.

The Queen smiled at me, raising her glass. "Cheers to your engagement, and cheers to new family."

I smiled back, pleasantly surprised by her sudden merriment. "Cheers." I sipped at the drink, trying to look graceful.

"I just wanted to let you know how happy I am for things to be working out." Andromeda lounged back comfortably against the armrest of the sofa.

"As am I, Your Majesty." It seemed as if I was starting to get on her good side.

"I assume it has been a very long day for you."

"Very much so," I agreed, setting my unfinished drink down on the windowsill next to where we sat.

"I don't want to keep you up, then." She rose from her seat. "Let me help you to bed."

Wow, this was really a change in character. "Um... thank you, Your Majesty, but we can call the Lady Minerva to help me, if that's preferable."

"Don't be ridiculous! I am here, and I am capable!" She immediately went to work on undoing my gown and sliding it off of me. She then moved to my wardrobe. "Would you like a nightgown?"

I stood still, trying to process what was happening. "Maybe I'll just sleep in my shift tonight."

"As you wish," she said, grabbing my hand and leading me to my bed. She began to pull the sheets and quilts over my body, just as a lady-in-waiting would. Out of the corner of my eye, I saw her slide a hand under the mattress for a second.

"What was that?" I asked.

"Oh, I was just tucking in a loose corner." She smiled down at me. "You know, I've always wanted a daughter."

The smile was warm, but then I noticed something... in her eyes, the same hint of amusement and glee King Leopold had in his eyes when he ordered Joseph's execution.

"What did you do?"
"Shhh…" she whispered.
And then I fell asleep.

Chapter 27

I woke up with my face on a hard, cold floor. I jumped up, surprised, and surveyed my surroundings. It seemed that I was in... a cell.

"Princess!"

I whirled my head around and saw Minerva in a cell next to mine. She was holding the metal bars adjoining the two, knuckles white from gripping them so tight.

"You've been asleep for so long! Nothing was waking you!"

I groaned, rubbing at a kink in my neck.

"She's awake," I heard a man's voice say. I turned my head in the direction of the voice.

"Hey!" I shouted. "What's going on?" Squinting my eyes in the dim lighting, I could see the figure of a guard sitting casually in a chair down the hallway.

"Answer me!" I said. No reply. "Minerva, do you know what happened? Why have we been arrested? Do they..." I lowered my voice, "know?"

She shrugged, tears spilling down her cheeks. I had never seen her such a mess."I have no idea. Shortly after the Queen asked me to leave you two alone, I went back to the party, and not ten minutes went by before I was hauled away by a couple of soldiers."

"The Queen!" I remembered. "She did something to me..."

The sound of footsteps came from the stairway, and Minerva and I looked eagerly in that direction, hoping for some possible answers. It was the Prince.

"Alexander!" I cried, quickly moving to the front of my cell and grabbing the bars. He didn't look at me, not even for a second. My heart sank to my stomach. "Alexander?"

He stood in front of me, eyes glued to the floor. His fists were clenched.

"We know you're not Princess Amelia," he said.

Minerva gasped. "How?" she exclaimed.

"Mother says she has sufficient evidence from some leaks in Mardasia," he said. Then he looked to Minerva. "Your outburst further proves it."

I shook my head, lip trembling. "Alexander, you have to believe me. I was forced—"

"Was it all I lie?" he shouted at me, eyes finally locking with mine. I jumped at the abruptness. "Everything? The fun we had, the stories we shared, our... our love?" He shifted his gaze to the floor again, shoving his clenched fists into his pockets.

"No!" I said. "Well, some of it was, but if you just let me explain..." I shot a glance at Minerva, but she did nothing to stop me. "Alexander, they forced me to do this. They've threatened me, and my sister."

"Why am I supposed to believe you?" he paced around, red in the face, and hit his fist against the wall.

I stared at him in pain, and my heart ached for him. And in that moment, I realized what he truly meant to me.

"Because I love you," I whispered. And I meant it this time. I loved his quirkiness, his kindness, his sense of humor...

Alexander sank to the floor and placed his face in his hands.

"It's true," Minerva spoke up.

We both turned to her, surprised. "The King, he threatened her, and I went along with it. The real Princess Amelia ran away, and we trained Milly here to replace her. When Milly tried to run away herself, the King killed her accomplice and threatened to do the same to her sister, who still lies in prison." Minerva looked to the floor, ashamed.

Alexander looked up at the ceiling and let out a long breath. "I don't know what to believe," he said, torment bleeding from his voice.

I rested my forehead against the bar, ignoring the cold. After a few minutes of silence, Alexander rose from the floor and turned to leave.

"Where are you going?" I croaked, holding back tears.

He froze in his path, but did not turn around. "I need to think," he said, then proceeded to leave.

I began to sob. My heart was at its breaking point. I curled up into a ball and allowed the despair to wash over me like a flood.

"I'm sorry, Milly," Minerva whispered.

Chapter 28

It was the dead of night, and I knew this scene all too well. Minerva and I sat, arms tied behind our backs, in front of Queen Andromeda as she sat regally in her throne. Her lips looked the color of blood against her ivory skin, and her eyes were squinted at us with displeasure. Alexander stood next to the throne, eyes at his feet and wringing his hands. My heart ached to see him that way.

"I would like to know just what your plan was," the Queen hissed at us.

I made eye contact with her, my lip trembling. "I don't know. My job was to keep up the farce to protect my sister." My voice croaked uncontrollably.

The Queen nodded to the guard behind me, the one who had been guarding mine and Minerva's cells for the last few hours, and he struck my cheek. I didn't even cry out.

"The Prince already informed me of that ridiculous story you claim!" Andromeda shouted, pounding her fist on the cushioned armrest of her throne. "I will give you one more chance, and you better tell the truth this time!"

I looked to Minerva for help, but she didn't provide any. She was pale as a sheet and shook violently.

"I don't know what to say," I whispered. "I never wanted this to happen. I never wanted to be here."

The guard struck me again, and this time I did cry out, my face already stinging from the last hit. Alexander made eye contact with me, a tear glistening on his cheek. I plead to him with my eyes.

"Mother," he said, "if they are telling the truth, they may be of use to us."

The Queen shot a glance at her son, then turned back to Minerva and me.

"What?" she spat.

Alexander nodded. "Obviously, King Leopold is a part of whatever plan this is, and I assume you would like for him to pay."

The Queen sat back, thoughtful. "There may be some merit to what you are saying, son."

We sat in a terrible silence as she pondered. Heavy thoughts ran through my head over and over again... My life seemed to always be in the hands of an angry, dictatorial monarch— no matter where I went.

"I'm going to strike a deal with the two of you."

Andromeda's words made me jump from the long silence.

"The only ones who know of your lies are in this room: myself, the Prince, and Ronald." The Queen nodded towards the guard standing behind us. "I will provide you with your lives if you cooperate."

Minerva nodded eagerly. "Anything, Your Majesty."

I hesitated. "What do you want us to do?"

Andromeda smiled, her eyes glinting with a morbid excitement. "We will pretend to go on with the wedding as planned. We will arrange an engagement tour of Polart and make our way to Mardasia, where the wedding is supposed to take place."

I tried to make eye contact with Alexander again to read his thoughts, but he kept his eyes on his mother.

The Queen continued. "And if neither of you interfere, my own plans for your dear King and Mardasia will take place." She raised an eyebrow at me, anticipating an interruption, but I stayed silent. "And your lives will be spared."

I stared out the large window in my bedchamber. Minerva was sleeping in her own room, exhausted by the ordeal. How did my life even get to this point? Sometimes I forgot how it happened, but this new turn of events was my best shot. If I still *pretended* to be Princess Amelia and *pretended* to go along with the wedding, I could still potentially save not only myself, but Janice, as well. But there was one problem: I was sick of pretending.

I rubbed my face with my hands. *Too much*, I thought. *This is too much.*

I wanted to see Alexander, talk to him, see what he was thinking, but I had hurt him, and that by itself was enough to drive me insane.

There was a sudden knock on my door, and I sighed. "Come in."

The young maid Clara pulled the door open and slipped through, timidly giving me a curtsy. "Princess, may I do some cleaning?"

I waved at her to proceed and she moved to my mattress to change the bedding.

"If I may, Your Highness, lots of us were worried about you yesterday. You weren't seen until this morning. Are you alright?" She kept her eyes on her work, too shy to look me in the eyes.

I smiled at her concern, then said what I was instructed to: "Lady Minerva and I decided to explore some of the Polart lands yesterday."

Clara seemed excited by that statement as she tore a sheet off the mattress. Before she could reply, however, something small flew out of the sheet and hit her in the eye, startling her.

"What was that?" She exclaimed.

I rushed over to find what had flown, curious.

"Oh, Princess!" Clara said, horrified. "Don't go crawling on the ground! I'll find it!"

But I had already located the object. "Is that a pea?" I said, holding it up so the maid could see.

The girl paled. "I'm so sorry, Your Highness! I must not have cleaned well enough last time."

I brushed it off. "Don't be ridiculous. It's just a little pea. It doesn't hurt anyone."

Chapter 29

The "wedding" was two weeks away, and we were starting the engagement tour. We were supposed to travel through the bigger part of Polart to make some public appearances, and then we would be doing the same in the Mardasia, arriving at the capital Capthar in time for the wedding. I was both dreading and looking forward to this tour. Dreading because it would be two weeks full of more lies. Looking forward because I would get to be with Alexander. I desperately wanted to talk to him.

I stood outside in a comfortable, yet elegant-looking travel dress, watching as various footmen and manservants packed up the party's luggage. It would be Alexander, the Queen, Lady Minerva, and me in the party, including the Lord and lady-in-waiting specifically going to fulfill the needs of the Prince and the Queen. And many soldiers, of course. As per Polart custom, the Queen would ride with her lady-in-waiting in a carriage at the front of the line, and Alexander and I would ride in a carriage behind with our own appointed companions, mine being Minerva. The entourage of soldiers would ride behind and around both carriages as a means of protection.

"I would've been excited for this," Minerva said beside me, "but now I just want everything to be over."

"I know what you mean." I looked at Minerva. She had been avoiding my eye contact all day and was much more jittery than normal— jumping at every little sound. Maybe she was just rattled by recent events.

All of the servants quieted and bowed. I turned around to see the Queen and Prince Alexander descending the steps of the castle's front entrance. I gave Alexander a smile, and he made eye contact with me. I saw the corners of his mouth lift a little in return. It wasn't much, but it was an improvement.

"Let's start!" the Queen said. She snapped her fingers for a footman to open her carriage door and help her inside. The fact that we were travelling for nearly two weeks was not reason enough for her to wear anything more practical: her blue skirts surrounded her in piles and piles of heavy fabric. The footman nearly had to push at her dress to make room inside the carriage for the Queen's travel companion.

As a courtesy, Alexander came up to me and held out his arm for me to take. I did and allowed him to help me into our carriage, Minerva next and Alexander's companion following behind.

I sat myself comfortably onto the seats, which

were so plush and soft that I sank an inch or two into them. Alexander took his seat next to me, and Minerva and the Lord across from us. My heart pounded at how close I sat to the Prince in the small compartment.

As soon as we were all settled inside, we felt the carriage lurch as it started on the path.

"Princess." Alexander's travel companion sitting next to Minerva got my attention. He was an extravagant-looking, older man with a curled mustache and long, dark bangs. He bowed his head in respect to me. "I am Lord William. It is an honor to meet you."

I bowed my head in return. "Likewise."

"This'll be so fun!" William exclaimed, bouncing up and down in his seat. Minerva eyed him, annoyed. He was definitely more... flamboyant than most men.

The ride consisted of William's many, *many* remarks about the countryside of Polart and "interesting" facts. No one else uttered a word. I had a hard time keeping my eyes open.

The first few stops were successful, but uneventful. We stopped in various-sized towns and were announced as the engaged Prince Alexander and Princess Amelia. The subjects of Polart were all so excited to see me. They're admiring eyes and cheerful applause made me feel sick.

At one stop I felt little hands pulling at my skirts. I whirled around to find a tiny girl, five or six, holding on to me, eyes wide in awe. It melted my heart. I crouched down to her level and moved the sweaty hair out of her face. She was dirty and poor, but a beautiful child.

"Hello," I said to her.

She gasped and turned a bright red. "Hello," she whispered timidly.

"What's your name?"

She shuffled her feet, but had a big smile on her face. "Molly." She giggled. "You a *beautiful* princess."

I found myself choking up. She was so innocent and looked up to me like a hero. "You are *also* a beautiful princess." I winked at her.

"Really?" She couldn't say her "r"s very well.

"Really."

Molly wrapped her arms around my neck, and I hugged her back. She ran off to tell her friends, I'm sure, and I stood up, brushing off my skirts.

"That was very sweet," Alexander whispered to me as we waved goodbye to the people at that particular stop.

"It was kind of hard, too," I replied. "I feel like I'm lying to *everybody*."

He watched my face, thoughtful.

I desperately wanted to talk with him— alone, but that entire week of travel did not give me any opportunity like that. The day came where we were to travel to Mardasia to make public appearances in some of the places there. I needed to find a time to pull Alexander aside before the end of that next week. I didn't know what would happen to me when Queen Andromeda's plan, whatever it was, followed through.

We sat in the carriage yet again, listening to William drone on and on.

"I've never actually been to the Kingdom of Mardasia before," he said, pressing his nose against the carriage window. "How far is it from here?"

"We're at the south edge of Polart right now. It'll take two or three days." Alexander lounged back in his seat and closed his eyes.

"Did you know that Mardasia's major export is metal?"

"Yes, Lord William!" Minerva snapped at him. "The Princess and I live there!"

"Oh…" William dejectedly shifted his gaze to his feet.

It was awkwardly silent for a moment, but Alexander broke the silence with laughter. I joined in, then Minerva, and then even Lord William started to chuckle.

"I'm sorry," the Lord said. "I know I'm a bit of a talker."

"That's alright, Lord William," the Prince said, wiping a tear from his eye from laughing so hard.

It had been a much needed laugh for all of us.

The sudden halt of the carriage woke me from my nap. Looking out the window, I saw that it was pitch black outside and assumed we were stopping to rest for the night. Our drivers, footmen, and soldiers, save the three who would be guarding our rooms in the inn, would be sleeping in the stables.

Upon entering the inn, the same thing that happened every night occured. People stared and whispered excitedly: men drunk from too many ales grinned ear to ear, the hired musician stopped playing his tune, and other guests slowly flocked in our direction. The three soldiers appointed to guard and protect us in the inn that night gently kept the crowd at bay.

We always stopped at the nicer inns during this trip, of course, but it didn't stop us from having to cohort with many, *many* subjects. As Milly the commoner, I didn't mind the people at all. But as the Princess, it got me too much attention.

"Silence!" the Queen cried, raising a gloved hand in the air. "We are exhausted from the day's journey, and we wish to retire. Lady Grisham, find the owner and procure us some rooms."

Andromeda gestured for her lady-in-waiting to follow her demands. After just a few seconds, the little woman came back with a robust, cheery man who hustled over to us, bowing over and over again.

"Oh, Your Majesty!" he said to the Queen. "And

Your Highnesses, Lord and Ladies. It is an honor to serve you!"

His bald head glistened as he sweated from the excitement and nerves.

"Thank you, Mr. Switch," Lady Grisham said. "We would like three of your best rooms please."

Mr. Switch grinned. "We do have a few rooms that are more expensive than the others."

"How much?" The Queen asked, digging a coin purse out of her travel cloak.

"Two silvers each room," he said, licking his lips.

The Queen pulled out a handful of gold coins from her bag. "Hmm…" she said. "No silver. Just keep all of this."

She handed him ten gold coins, and his eyes bugged out of his head.

"Thank you, Your Majesty!" he exclaimed, bowing again.

The Queen waved her hand, dismissing it. "Oh, bother. It's just money."

It took everything I had in me not to roll my eyes. She did this every stop. It was like she *enjoyed* throwing and flaunting her riches at people.

Mr. Switch began to waddle up the large staircase at the end of the room, gesturing for us to follow. I surveyed the room as we climbed the wooden stairs, enjoying the warmth from the giant fire burning in the hearth in the dining room. Most people were still watching us, contemplating how they would tell their friends and family who they saw that night. The musician began playing his lute and singing again, and the servers went around delivering food to their guests. One of the servers looked familiar to me, and I halted on the staircase for a second to study her more. Long, blonde curls fell to her waist, and she laughed with a man as she poured him another drink. She turned around and caught sight of me staring at her.

I gasped. "You!"

The rose in her cheeks faded as she went pale, nearly dropping the pitcher in her hands. Minerva, obviously not seeing the girl, urged me to continue up the stairs. The young woman scurried out of the dining room. I wanted to chase after her, but knew it would make too much of a scene.

It was her, I thought. *It was Princess Amelia.*

Chapter 30

The silence of the night was too much to bear. It allowed all of my thoughts to come to the surface. I lay awake in bed, tossing and turning. I didn't think I would ever see Princess Amelia again, not after that fateful night when Janice and I had helped her escape Mardasia.

Minerva was sound asleep in the bed next to mine. I was *not* going to tell her who I had seen, in fear of how she would react. There was only one person who could help me.

I swung my legs off the mattress and marched over to my door.

"Guard," I said, swinging the door open.

The man jumped, then saluted. He seemed to have been falling asleep. "Princess Amelia!"

"I wish to speak with the Prince."

"Uh…" He seemed at a loss for words.

"Now," I demanded. "It's urgent."

The man scratched his head in confusion, but led me across the hall to the Prince's room. The guard stationed there perked up as he saw us approach.

"Your Highness." He bowed. He was much

smaller than his colleague.

"The Princess wishes to speak to Prince Alexander," my guard said to him.

The other man cocked his head to the side. "In the dead of night?"

"Yes," I replied. "Please alert him."

He shrugged and knocked on the Prince's door. Alexander answered within seconds— he must've been awake, too. The sight of me in my nightgown made him blush.

"We need to talk," I said as I pushed past the two guards before they could say anything.

Lord William startled from his sleep as I entered the room.

"What's going on?" He sat up quickly, rubbing his eyes.

"Lord William," I said politely, "I have an urgent matter to discuss with His Highness. Could you leave us alone for just a little while?"

The Lord coughed. "Is that wise?"

"We'll be fine." Alexander encouraged him to leave, obviously curious.

"Shut the door behind you!" I called out to Lord William as he left.

The door clicked shut, and I began pacing the floor, trying to gather my thoughts.

"Amelia, what's going on?" He sat down at the desk in the room. A candle was still lit— he had been reading before I interrupted.

I shook my head. "Please, if I could hear someone call me by my real name just *once*, I would be so grateful!"

"Um…" He paused for a long time. "What was it again?"

That was it. I broke down into tears and slumped onto his bed. He rose in concern and slowly approached me, not sure what to do.

"I'm going to talk, and you are going to listen," I said. Alexander seemed taken aback, but he slowly sat back down.

I took a deep breath. "My name is Mildred Wallander. I am from a small town in Mardasia, and up until recently, I lived with my sister Janice after our mother died and our drunk father left."

And then I continued on with my whole story: I told him of the surprise visit from Princess Amelia all those nights ago. I angrily explained the appalling nature of how I was kidnapped and forced to train as the new Princess Amelia. I sobbed some more as I told him of Joseph and our unsuccessful escape, leading to his death and my sister's imprisonment. I went through every threat King Leopold had said to me as I had no choice but to continue with my farce and marry the Prince of Polart, and how, against all odds, I fell in love with him.

"I am so tired of pretending!" I kept quiet enough so those outside couldn't hear, but I wanted to scream. "But the one thing that has gotten me though *any* of it is you."

Alexander had taken a seat next to sometime during my monologue, and I hadn't noticed until he slipped his arms around me and pulled me into a warm hug. I melted into his arms and pressed my nose into his neck.

"Mildred," he whispered.

"Milly," I interrupted. "No one calls me Mildred."

He grabbed my face in his hands and wiped my tears away.

"Whatever your name is, whoever you are, it doesn't matter."

I stared into his eyes, which were filling with tears of their own. He wasn't wearing his glasses at the moment, and I had never noticed the little flecks of blue sparkling in his green eyes before. He continued:

"What I do know is this: I fell in love with you, and nothing will ever change that."

He kissed me. I slid my fingers into his hair and kissed him back. I truly did need this man, and he believed me... and he loved me. Knowing that felt better than I could've possibly imagined.

"I've missed you," he whispered. "I'm so sorry I didn't believe you at first."

We held each other, and I could've stayed like that forever, but there was more he needed to know.

"She's here," I said. "The real Princess Amelia. I saw her."

"What?" Alexander grabbed my shoulders. "Where? When?"

"Downstairs," I whispered. "She was serving

food and drink to guests— she was working. And she recognized me."

He rubbed his face with his hand. "Wow. What do we do?"

I shook my head. "Nothing. We shouldn't give her away. She's lucky to have gotten away from her father and that life."

"But she ended up giving *her* life to *you*!"

"It wasn't her fault." I looked down at my hands and at the engagement ring on my finger. "Besides, I would have never met you." I smiled up at him, and he couldn't help but smile back.

There was a knock at the door, and Lord William peeked his head in.

"Are you two alright?"

Alexander turned to the door. He was really quick on his feet. "The Princess was just feeling a bit unwell from all of this travelling and had trouble sleeping."

"I'm sorry, Princess Amelia." William bowed his head. "Um, I was wondering if I could have my bed back now?"

I chuckled a bit. "My apologies, Lord William."

"No worries!" he said, eagerly making his way back to his mattress. "I hope you start feeling better, Princess."

I glanced at Alexander as I left the room. I really *was* starting to feel better.

Chapter 31

As we left that morning, I couldn't find Amelia anywhere. Seeing me must have spooked her. I was happy for her— truly. She had gotten away, and I didn't spite her one bit. Whatever she was doing with her life, I hoped she was happy.

The rest of the trip was considerably more comfortable after having reconciled with Alexander. He held my hand most of the way, not caring about what Minerva and William would think. But the impending end to the journey was scaring me. Queen Andromeda had planned for our party to travel through Mardasia before arriving at the castle in Capthar, making various public appearances on the way. I was nervous for that, thinking that someone was bound to recognize that I wasn't the Princess Amelia in my own kingdom, but no one seemed to notice. I had long, blonde hair like the real Princess, and I was kept far enough away from the crowds. The lack of outbursts that I was a fake eased my mind some, but I was still worried about arriving to the castle. Who knew what Queen Andromeda had up her sleeve? All I wanted was for it to be over and to find Janice.

We were about a day's travel away from the castle, and Alexander watched as I wrung my hands. He stopped me with his own hands and squeezed.

I glanced over at Minerva and William. They were sound asleep, Minerva's head dangerously close to falling on William's shoulder.

"Will my life ever be normal again?" I whispered back to him.

"You weren't made for 'normal.'"

"What is that supposed to mean?" I teased.

Alexander blushed. "I meant it as a compliment."

I nudged his shoulder playfully. "I know."

I hesitated, not sure if voicing my next thoughts was a smart thing to do, but I did anyway: "What does your mother have planned for Mardasia?"

Alexander paled and looked intensely at the two in front of us, making sure they really were asleep.

"I don't know if we should be talking about that right now."

I lowered my voice even more, feeling the same anxiety he felt. "When *will* we talk about it, Alexander?"

He rested his face in his palms. "She's attacking Mardasia in secret, while we go in for the wedding celebrations as a distraction."

I nodded, expecting as much.

"You're not surprised?"

"It makes sense," I whispered back. "Our kingdoms have been on the brink of war for years, and our marriage was supposed to help settle that. King Leopold pulling this 'fake Amelia' stunt probably pushed things over the edge."

Alexander snorted. "That's for sure."

I rested my head on his shoulder, exhausted from the fear and anticipation.

"No matter what," Alexander breathed in my ear, "I won't leave your side." He kissed the top of my head, and all of my worries dissipated.

We arrived in Capthar the day before the date of the wedding. King Leopold didn't give us much time before he announced we were all to attend a dinner in celebration of the impending nuptials. After hurriedly getting bathed and dressed, I found myself sitting next to the King at the large dining table I had eaten at many times before. Alexander and Queen Andromeda sat across from me, Minerva and Lord William next, then what seemed to be dozens upon dozens of nobles not just from Mardasia, but from Polart, as well.

Everyone was cheerily drinking and eating as they celebrated Prince Alexander's and my union that was supposed to happen tomorrow morning. Alexander picked at his food, seemingly unable to eat more than a couple bites. He always felt awkward around lots of people. Queen Andromeda, however, was smiling. It never faltered. She watched King Leopold carefully as he boisterously spoke to everyone in the room, laughing and being the most cheerful I had ever seen him. It wasn't fake, he was truly happy this wedding was happening. But I knew something he didn't: Queen Andromeda's army should be taking the Mardasian borders any second now, and I found myself waiting for *something* to happen as each second passed by.

"Daughter!" Leopold said, startling me. "Why do you look so glum? This is a joyous occasion!"

All eyes in the room were on me. The Queen, Alexander, Leopold, Minerva, and the nobles of Mardasia all knew of my true identity, but there were many in the room who did not.

"Maybe she is nervous about the wedding night!" a wrinkled, plump old lady from Polart shouted.

Everybody in the room burst out laughing, all drunk from the alcohol they had consumed. They slapped each other's backs and cheered the Prince and me on. I flushed a deep red and found myself sinking into my chair a little. Alexander didn't handle the jeers any better than I could.

"Well, my girl, put a smile on that beautiful face." The King winked at me, and I shuddered at the sight.

"Forgive me, Sire," I said, feigning a laugh. "I was

just deep in thought, I guess."

Queen Andromeda's eyes were on me as she sliced through the beef on her plate. It felt as if the knife were slicing through me. She shook her head ever so slightly. "Don't you dare say anything," her look read.

I took another bite of my own food, completely desensitized to any taste at all. Time ticked away in slow motion. As I chewed my food, I caught sight of some dark eyes staring at me from behind a banister in the corner of the room. Squinting my eyes to get a better look, I nearly shouted from fright. The woman grinned at me with her rotted teeth as she twirled one of the few tufts of her gray hair on her finger. This time I recognized her. I had seen her before, not just on my first day in Polart, but that day in Marviton! I had given her some apples. How could I forget? And Minerva had called her a witch. I thought back to the day she said things no one could possibly know, like how I helped the Princess Amelia escape. And then I remembered her vanishing into thin air as quickly as she had come. Magic...

The witch lifted a knobby finger to her lips, urging me to be quiet. The look in her eyes was playful, and she did a little shimmy with her shoulders. I must have blinked, because in a split second, she was gone.

"A toast!" King Leopold bellowed to the room, lifting his glass of wine.

Silence fell as everyone lifted their glasses in return. I shook my head, reaching for my own glass. It had to be the stress playing tricks on my mind.

"To the union of Princess Amelia and Prince Alexander! And to the union of the kingdoms of Mardasia and Polart!"

"Here, here!" the many voices at the table shouted. Many around gulped their drinks down while I merely took a sip.

"Ugh!" Queen Andromeda exclaimed. Everyone looked at her. "There's a pea in my cup!"

A pea?

The Queen's eyes grew wide as she grabbed at her throat, beginning to choke. Many rose from their seats to see what was happening.

"Mother?" Alexander cried, grabbing at her hand. "Mother!"

Alexander leaped from his seat, but before he could help her, the life in her forest green eyes faded, and we watched in horror as her face fell straight into the potatoes on her plate. There was an outburst of panicked screams, and I sat with my mouth hanging open as I stared at Andromeda's corpse.

"What did you do?" Alexander rushed at King Leopold, grabbing him by the collar in a sudden fury.

The King's soldiers immediately pulled Alexander away, and others surrounded the few Polart soldiers before they could move to help their Prince.

Leopold straightened his shirt, laughing. "I'm

surprised that your mother thought she could outsmart me," he said.

"What are you talking about?" Alexander spat. His glasses fell off his face while he struggled. They shattered as they hit the floor.

I moved towards Alexander, but I was grabbed by some more Mardasian soldiers from behind. The nobles in the room stayed silent, fearing the soldiers surrounding them with pointed swords and spears.

King Leopold stood, addressing everybody in the room. "I know she found out that dear Princess Amelia here isn't *really* dear Princess Amelia after all." The Polart nobles in the room gasped while the Mardasians lowered their eyes to the floor.

"That's right!" the King shouted, still laughing. "My daughter ran away, so I replaced her with this trash!" He pointed in my direction. "Queen Andromeda learned of the plan and secretly sent an army here to take over while she *herself* pretended to keep going along with this wedding!" He smiled, eyes glowing with a determined fire. "Her pathetic army lay dead at our borders."

"How?" Alexander cried. "How did you find out?"

Lady Minerva slowly rose from her seat and moved to stand by the King's side.

"My people always stay loyal."

Minerva avoided my gaze. My thoughts churned as to how she could have possibly contacted him without my knowledge.

"And you." The King's voice grew scarily softer as he turned to me. "You have always been and always will be a disappointment." He looked to one of the guards by the entryway of the dining hall. "Kill the sister."

"No!" I shouted, squirming helplessly against the strong grip of the men behind me.

Alexander was fuming and somehow ripped himself away from his captors.

"I challenge you!" he shouted.

Everyone froze, including the man sent to kill Janice. After the initial moment of shock, the soldiers moved in to restrain the Prince again, but Leopold raised his hand to stop them.

"Interesting," the King said, stroking his bearded chin. "At what stakes, if I may ask?"

Alexander looked at me. I shook my head, terrified.

Don't do this, I thought.

"If you win, you do whatever you want to all of us, and Polart is yours," Alexander said. The crowd gasped. "But if I win, both Mardasia and Polart are mine. And Milly, her sister, and everyone else go free."

Leopold grinned, seemingly amused by the Prince's offer. "I accept your challenge."

Chapter 32

King Leopold ordered for space to made, planning to duel the Prince right there in the dining hall. I watched wordlessly as the Queen's body was whisked away, then the table was quickly moved to the side. People scurried nervously to the edges of the room, and I was dragged along with them.

"Weapons?" the King asked.

Alexander shrugged. "You choose."

"Swords then! Simple, but requires significant skill."

With a snap of the King's finger, a couple of soldiers withdrew their swords and presented them to the fighters.

"To the death?" Leopold was grinning.

Alexander nodded. "To the death."

I was in shock. I knew Alexander was a good swordsman, but King Leopold had his own reputation— he was one of the best. And to top it all off, Alexander didn't have his glasses. He was going to get himself killed!

"Do not interfere!" the King shouted to his soldiers in the room. "I've been needing something fun like this for a long time."

Leopold struck first, but Alexander parried the blow and danced around the King. Too fast for my eyes to see, the Prince struck and nicked the King's arm. Leopold didn't even look at the cut and chuckled a bit.

"You are very quick, Prince."

Alexander stood defensively, sword outstretched from his body, and didn't reply. The King struck again, but Alexander spun the sword off of his, making the King stumble. He steadied himself quickly, then struck again. Alexander stepped to the side and sliced his blade through the King's other arm. The cut was deeper this time.

It was amazing. The Prince made the King look like a novice. The crowd watched in anticipated silence as strike after strike hit. Alexander cut up the King on very limb. It was like he wasn't delivering a fatal blow on purpose, having had many opportunities to do so.

The King was getting angry. Blood dripped at his wobbling feet as he tried to steady his sword hand. The two faced each other, waiting for the other to make another move.

"You're pathetic!" the King spat. "You will *never* amount to anything! You're just an awkward, little boy who can't get anywhere without his mother!"

Alexander clenched his fists. "I'm not the one covered in blood from fighting this so-called little boy!"

The King shifted his gaze up to the ceiling and started to laugh maniacally.

"You don't know anything!" the King exclaimed. "Your mother lied to you your whole life!"

"What are you talking about?" Alexander spat back.

"You never wondered as to how your father died so young and healthy? She killed him! She only ever wanted the power."

There was an outburst of chatter among the people in the room, and all eyes were on Prince Alexander. He didn't move. I definitely had thought the Queen to be scary and intense, but killing her own husband?

"And she was going to sabotage your marriage to Princess Amelia no matter what. She was just lucky that the Princess turned out to be an impostor!"

Alexander's hands fell to his side, and the tip of his sword clinked against the stone floor.

"Your mother was dirt!"

"Shut up," Alexander whispered.

The King cupped a bloodied hand around his ear. "I couldn't quite hear. Was that a mouse? Must have been, because I don't see a man in front of me."

"Shut up!" Alexander shouted.

He leaped towards the King, too fast for him to react, and grabbed him into a chokehold.

Many of the Mardasian soldiers moved to help their King.

"Stay back!" Alexander ordered. "Or I will slice his throat!" He yanked Leopold's hair back with his free hand, exposing the white skin under the King's beard.

King Leopold began to whimper. I found myself smiling at the fear in his eyes.

"Please," Leopold croaked. "I yield!"

"Relinquish your kingdom to me," Alexander said, pressing the cold blade a little harder onto the King's neck. "And leave immediately, leaving Milly, me, and everyone else alone forever!"

"Anything!" the King cried. He trembled like helpless prey. "I'll do anything!"

The Prince tossed the King aside in disgust, and turned his back to him, facing the crowd.

The Polartians cheered and bowed to their Prince in respect. The Mardasians were more reluctant, but they bowed, as well. The soldiers behind me released me from their grip, and I ran to Alexander, but was stopped in my tracks. There she was again... the witch. She was giggling behind the same banister and pointed at the King.

"Look out!" I shouted to Alexander.

King Leopold had picked up his blade and attempted a final blow towards his enemy. Alexander tried to dodge it, but was too slow as the sword nicked his shoulder. But his next move was quicker. Without any hesitation, Alexander grabbed the King by the back of the head and thrust his sword into Leopold's gut.

The King coughed up some dribbles of blood as he fell to his knees.

"No," he whispered. His eyes caught mine as his body began to convulse. "No…"

Leopold's body slumped to the floor, and just like that, I was free.

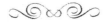

Bavmorda slipped away from the noisy crowd after King Leopold's lifeless body hit the floor. No one noticed her walk away as she stayed to the shadows, including that fake Princess. Bavmorda watched as the girl and the Prince held each other in a tearful, relieved embrace.

Ah, love, she thought.

Bavmorda flipped the tattered hood of her cloak over her balding head and made her way out of the castle. She had finished the job she needed to do. The Queen had needed to pay her price for the magic Bavmorda had given her a couple weeks ago, and King Leopold seeking her out to help kill the Queen was just icing on the cake. The poisoned pea in the wine was hilarious and rather ironic, some of her best work. And the King ended up paying his price a lot sooner than Bavmorda thought he would, so that was nice.

The witch sighed. Where to next? She had heard of a peasant girl in a distant land desperately wanting to go to a ball for some reason. Or maybe she should monitor how many poisoned apples were flying about in that one kingdom? The possibilities were endless, but at the moment, she was glad of her successes with helping Mildred Wallander find a happily ever after.

Chapter 33

I sighed in relief when I found Alexander sitting on the grass of King Leopold's grounds, picking at the blades and clenching them in his fists. It had been a couple hours since the duel, and things were a little chaotic and panicked in the castle at the moment. The people outside had yet to be told of King Leopold's demise, but that could wait. After having found Janice, I had noticed Alexander's disappearance and thought it important to find him.

"Alexander?" I said.

Not caring about the expensive silk of my dress, I moved to sit by him on the moist ground. I placed my hand on his arm.

"My mother was many things," he croaked, "but I never thought she could..." He tried to hide the tears that began to spill from his eyes.

Tears of my own formed as I felt his pain. I wrapped my arms around him.

"He was so young," he continued. "And there was evidence of foul play, but we never solved the mystery." He lifted his face to mine, his tears intensifying the green in his eyes. "So it makes sense." He slid himself away from my grip and sat up straighter. "A part of me almost suspected it, but I never wanted to believe it."

He turned his face up to the sky and chuckled slightly.

"It almost feels nice," he said.

That confused me. "What feels nice?"

"That she's gone." He glanced at me to see my reaction, but I just nodded. "I loved my mother, but she never allowed me to be who I needed to be."

"You feel free."

"Exactly." He smiled at me. "However, I can't think about that right now. There are too many things to be done."

He stood up from his position and rolled his shoulders back. I gazed up at him, admiring the strength and courage in his face, a stark difference from the sad boy seconds ago. Now he was a man adopting the demeanor of a king.

"First thing's first." He turned to me, the sun glinting off his blond hair, making it hard for me to see his face. "Milly, may I have your ring?"

My heart dropped. Was this it? I guess he couldn't marry a commoner after all. It wouldn't make sense. I stood up, trying to keep my lip from trembling, and slid the gold band off my left hand.

He grabbed it from me and stared at it for a moment, then dropped down on one knee. I jumped back for a second, confused.

"What are you doing?"

"Mildred Wallander, if you mess up *another* proposal, I will never talk to you again."

I found myself beaming, and then laughter spilled out of me. I found myself unable to stop. Alexander started laughing, too.

"Milly," he said between laughs, "stop it! I can't breathe."

I finally was able to reel myself back in, wiping tears away from my eyes. He outstretched one hand to me, still kneeling, and I took it in my own.

"Milly, from the first moment I watched you climb that tree, I fell in love with you. Not Princess Amelia, *you*. You are beautiful, funny, kind, and brave. I cannot imagine my life without you." He held the engagement ring closer to me. "Will you marry me? For real this time?"

I squealed and threw myself into his arms, making him lose his balance. We fell into the grass, laughing and kissing.

He grabbed my face in his hands. "You still haven't said 'yes.'"

"Yes!" I cried.

Alexander's face fell, and he gasped. "Wait! I dropped the ring! It's in the grass somewhere."

So, on our hands and knees, we searched for the ring, laughing enough for an entire lifetime. Even though it took us maybe a half an hour to find it, those were some of the best minutes of my life.

Chapter 34

Alexander and I sat at one of the many tables in the dining room of the inn. The many guests around us were staring and whispering things like, "That's King Alexander and his wife Queen Mildred," And, "What a handsome couple!" Or, "What on earth are they doing eating breakfast at a place like this?" But no one approached us. We were making it very clear that we weren't there to socialize.

"Are you sure she's here?"

"I'm not sure she would *still* be here, but this is where I saw her," I whispered back to him.

And then it happened. Princess Amelia bustled out of the kitchen with trays of food piled on her arms. Her cheeks were red from the exertion, and her pretty hair was frizzed up about an inch away from her head.

"That's her!" I said excitedly.

We watched as Amelia delivered the food in her arms, smiling kindly at the people as she did so. She really did seem happy. She made eye contact with me and gasped, but she didn't move to get away. I waved her down, and she hesitantly approached our table.

"Your Majesties," she said, curtsying. Her curtsies were much more graceful than those of the common folk, for obvious reasons.

Alexander dismissed the gesture. "There is no need for that."

"We need to talk," I said.

People watched curiously as Alexander and I led Amelia to a private room we had rented for just this purpose. After shutting the door behind us, Alexander and I did our own bowing.

"Princess Amelia," we said simultaneously.

She paled. "Are you here to turn me in?"

I rose from my curtsy and smiled. "Do you still have my horse?"

Amelia studied for a moment, obviously confused, but then her eyes lit up.

"Of course! That's why I recognized you!" She rushed over and threw her arms around me in a hug.

"Thank you," she said. She released me from her grip and began to wipe the tears from her eyes. "You have no idea what gift you gave me." She started laughing. "How on earth did you end up married to the Prince I was engaged to?"

Alexander and I shared knowing glances.

"It's a very long story." I chuckled. "You might want to sit down."

Amelia raised an eyebrow at me and sat on one of the wooden chairs against the wall.

"Well, I'm definitely curious," she said, gesturing for us to begin.

And so we did. Her eyes grew wider and wider as she learned of her father's plans to turn me into a fake Princess Amelia and marry me to the Prince. Her mouth hung open as we told her of Queen Andromeda's death and King Leopold's own demise by Alexander's hands.

We waited nervously for her to say something, anything. Then she finally did:

"I knew my father had died, but I thought... I didn't know all of that happened." She looked to Alexander. "And now you rule over both Mardasia and Polart?"

He nodded. "For now..."

"Are you okay?" I asked Amelia, reaching over to put my hand on hers.

"I don't know what to feel," she whispered. "My father obviously was not a good man, but..." She shook her head. "It doesn't matter. It's not my life anymore."

"Well..." I said.

Amelia perked up and urged us to tell her what we weren't saying.

"I don't want to rule Mardasia," Alexander said. "I earned the kingdom through malice and anger, and that is not right, no matter how terrible King Leopold was."

I chimed in. "You are still the King's heir." I squeezed Amelia's hands in mine. "We are hoping you can assume the throne and rebuild Mardasia into something great again."

Amelia stood up quickly, releasing her hands from mine. "But I have a life here! I have a home, and my husband and I... we're expecting a new baby!"

"You're married?" I said.

"You're pregnant?" Alexander exclaimed.

I thought back to the rumors of the Princess running away with a servant boy

Amelia began pacing the floor. "What would the people think?"

"They would be grateful for a kind monarch they know they could stand behind," I assured her.

We waited in silence as Amelia continued to pace. I was surprised she wasn't wearing a hole into the carpet.

"Can I think about it?"

Alexander was about to protest, but I shook my head at him.

"Take all the time you need," I said.

It had been days since our visit to the Princess Amelia, and we were starting to lose any hope. Alexander and I were pouring over maps of both Polart and Mardasia in our library, making various plans to efficiently rule over both kingdoms. At the moment, we had an appointed Lord residing in

Capthar to keep the chaos at bay as we tried to determine what our next step should be.

A knock sounded on the door, and one of our manservants entered the room.

"Your Majesties," he said, bowing his head. "Princess Amelia of Mardasia is here to address you."

Alexander and I gave each other a look, and then watched as Amelia stepped into the library, a very handsome young man at her side. We exchanged curtsies and bows to one another before any of us spoke.

"King Alexander, Queen Mildred, this is my husband Robert." Amelia pointed to the man beside her.

"Robert," Alexander said. "It is a pleasure to meet you."

"Likewise, Your Majesty." He seemed very confident and regal for a servant boy.

"I have made my decision."

Alexander and I leaned forward, awaiting her next words.

"I will rule as Queen of Mardasia with Robert at my side. It is my duty, and my people need me."

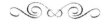

Amelia and her husband stood in front of the

masses of people in the throne room of Capthar as a priest dressed in long robes anointed them as Mardasia's new rulers. The people had accepted the true return of their Princess with open arms, and she had already done so much work repairing the kingdom. She had been making regular visits to every city and town in Mardasia to help ease the minds of her subjects and assure them that she was there to help. She even took notes on what the people wanted to see from her— lower taxes, the rebuilding of aging roads... I had never seen someone work as kindly and efficiently as Amelia did.

It had been a few weeks since Amelia had agreed to take her place as Queen, so her expectant belly was a little more obvious as she knelt when the priest instructed her to. I smiled. She looked absolutely beautiful.

Janice sat beside me, tears spilling from her eyes as she listened to the priest's inspiring words.

"Announcing Queen Amelia and King Robert of Mardasia!" an announcer bellowed.

The crowd rose from their seats and roared. Amelia and Robert rose from their knees and smiled at the cheers.

"What are you thinking?" Alexander whispered in my ear as he interlocked his fingers with mine.

"That I would have never guessed it."

"Guessed what?"

I smiled up at him and gave him a tender kiss. "That I would be so lucky."

Note from the Author

Thank you for taking the time to read my book! I hope you enjoyed it. If you did, spreading the word would be much appreciated! For instance, leaving an Amazon or Goodreads review, or sharing on social media, would make all the difference!

Subscribe to my newsletter and take a look at my website to receive updates, book releases, and so much more!

Newsletter: http://eepurl.com/g-ioqz
Site: https://aleesehughes.com

Be sure to follow me on all social medias:

Instagram: @aleesehughes
Facebook: Aleese Hughes
Twitter: @AleeseHughes

Sneak Peek...

Apples and Princesses

Chapter 1

I rubbed my arm, wincing at the pain. The bruise was already starting to form. I clenched my jaw and wiped at the hot tears spilling down my cheeks. My father's abuse didn't make me sad anymore—it made me angry.

I pushed through the trees and ran faster, not knowing where I was going. All I knew was that I just wanted to run. I often found solitude in the woods after a particularly bad bout of temper from Father, but it had just been particularly bad. He struck me more than once, and I didn't know how much more I could take. I was beginning to reach my threshold of tolerance.

My father was a rich lord with a manor in the country, and his land went on for miles, so I had no idea of knowing how far I had to go before I could be free. But did I want to leave? What would I do; where would I go?

Shaking my head, I stopped, staring up at the night sky past the bright green leaves of the forest. The wind chilled me, and I regretted running out into the night wearing only a thin, short-sleeved gown.

"Hello, child."

I jumped at the voice, whirling around to see a ragged old woman with little gray hair left on her head. Her teeth weren't much better. In her arms, she held a large wicker basket full of red apples. The skin of the fruit gleamed underneath the moonlight.

"Who are you?" I squeaked, inching away from the woman.

The woman licked her chapped lips and smiled. "I've been going by Bavmorda lately, and I rather like that name."

Bavmorda started stepping towards me, seemingly desensitized to the sharp branches under her bare feet. I gagged at the sight of her long, yellowed toenails.

"And you, my dear, skin as white as snow, lips the color of blood, hair as black as ebony... You must be Snow White."

I cocked my head, not knowing whether to feel nervous or curious. Magic was a common practice in the Edristan Kingdom, and I had met a few magicians and fortune tellers in the past, but it was not always a respected practice.

"Are you a witch?"

Bavmorda cackled, her throat moving like a

croaking toad's. "That's one way to label what I do." She moved even closer. "I've wanted to meet you."

I didn't move away from the woman this time. "Why?"

Bavmorda shrugged clumsily, the basket still in her arms. "I have seen that our paths will cross many times in the future."

That made me laugh, and the sound of my voice echoed around us. "Is that so?"

I knew fortune tellers to be more tricksters than to have actual, supernatural foresight. At least, the few that traveled to the Manor for Father's entertainment gave me that impression. The witch knew my name, but anyone could have a lucky guess. Maybe she inquired after the White family before... Or perhaps she knew of White Manor and its inhabitants.

"I know what you're thinking." Bavmorda set the basket down and stretched out her back. I winced at the sound of many joints and bones popping all at once. "Let me prove my abilities to you." She wiggled her knobby fingers and grinned. "Your mother wanted to name you Snow because of your beautiful, fair skin and rather liked how it fit with the surname of 'White.' Unfortunately, your mother died due to complications of your birth, and your father hasn't been the same ever since."

In the blink of an eye, Bavmorda came up to me and grabbed my bruised arm. "Your father's insanity tends to cause you some unwarranted pain, if I'm correct in saying so." She clicked her tongue. "How sad."

I pulled my arm away from the witch's grasp, then immediately regretted the brash movement against my bruises.

"How—"

Bavmorda rolled her dark eyes and sighed. "People always ask me 'how.' I'm a witch, that should be enough explanation."

Despite the woman's unnatural ability of "knowing things," I didn't find myself scared.

"Why all the apples?"

"Oh, those!" Bavmorda looked at her basket in disgust. "I confiscated those from a lowly warlock in town. He thinks it's okay to give out poisoned apples like candy." She put her hands on her hips. "He thinks it's funny."

My curiosity came to its peak.

"Poisoned apples?" I said, moving to touch one.

Bavmorda placed herself in between me and the basket. "What do you think you're doing?"

I crinkled my nose at the witch's pungent breath. "Sorry."

"You shouldn't be playing with these," Bavmorda spat. "One bite can put someone into an almost permanent coma. More than that will kill."

She pulled her holey shawl back over her shoulders, shivering in the night air and pulled the basket back into her grasp with a grunt.

"Until next time, child."

I watched as the woman hobbled away. Then, out of nowhere, one of the apples rolled from the top and fell onto the forest floor. The witch didn't seem to notice. I waited until Bavmorda was out of sight and rushed to grab it.

I looked at the deep red apple against my white hands and slid my fingernails along the hard skin. It was one of the most delicious-looking apples I had ever seen. My thoughts started turning. I didn't completely believe that someone in town would just be giving out lethal produce. On the other hand, if Bavmorda had been telling the truth, I might be able to get some use out of this apple. I thought of my abusive father. But would I? Would I even be able to follow through with it?

I tucked my hands and the apple away at the front of my purple, silk skirts and closed my eyes. The breeze blew through my dark hair that flowed undone past my hips, and a smile formed on my blood-red lips. There was no harm in trying.

Want to read more? Read *Apples and Princesses* now!

Map

About the Author

Aleese Hughes is many things: a mother and wife, an avid reader, a performer, and an author. Aleese enjoys her time at home with her children and relishes the opportunities to pick up a good book or write one herself.

Having grown up around theater her entire life, Aleese has a natural ability when it comes to charming audiences while on stage. And the same goes for her knack to put words to paper and create stories that people of all ages can read and enjoy.

The fantasy genre is not only her favorite to read, but it is also what she writes, including "The Tales and Princesses Series," and "After the Tales and Princesses- A Set of Novellas."

More by Aleese Hughes

The Tales and Princesses Series

Book 1: Peas and Princesses

Book 2: Apples and Princesses

Book 3: Pumpkins and Princesses

Book 4: Beasts and Princesses

After the Tales and Princesses — A Set of Novellas

Novella 1: Janice Wallander: A Novella Retelling the Tale of Rumpelstiltskin

Novella 2: Queen Dalia Char: A Novella Retelling the Tale of Rose Red

Made in the USA
Columbia, SC
04 June 2021